"What's wrong?" Sasha asked.

"Maybe nothing," Bradley responded, but King didn't growl without a good reason. "Stay here. I'm going to check things out."

"But–" she began.

He didn't have time to explain or reassure. "Stay here," he repeated, leaving the apartment and running downstairs.

King's ears perked, his scruff still raised as he sniffed the air. He growled, his attention focused on the house across the street, its yard dotted with large bushes.

Someone was there.

TRUE BLUE K-9 UNIT: BROOKLYN

*These police officers fight for justice
with the help of their brave canine partners.*

Aside from her faith and her family, there's not much **Shirlee McCoy** enjoys more than a good book! When she's not hanging out with the people she loves most, she can be found plotting her next Love Inspired Suspense story or trekking through the wilderness, training with a local search-and-rescue team. Shirlee loves to hear from readers. If you have time, drop her a line at shirlee@shirleemccoy.com.

Books by Shirlee McCoy

Love Inspired Suspense

True Blue K-9 Unit: Brooklyn

Delayed Justice

FBI: Special Crimes Unit

Night Stalker
Gone
Dangerous Sanctuary
Lone Witness
Falsely Accused

Mission: Rescue

Protective Instincts
Her Christmas Guardian
Exit Strategy
Deadly Christmas Secrets
Mystery Child
The Christmas Target
Mistaken Identity
Christmas on the Run

Visit the Author Profile page at Harlequin.com for more titles.

DELAYED JUSTICE

SHIRLEE MCCOY

LOVE INSPIRED SUSPENSE
INSPIRATIONAL ROMANCE

Special thanks and acknowledgment are given to Shirlee McCoy for her contribution to the True Blue K-9 Unit: Brooklyn miniseries.

LOVE INSPIRED® SUSPENSE

INSPIRATIONAL ROMANCE

Recycling programs
for this product may
not exist in your area.

ISBN-13: 978-1-335-57470-1

Delayed Justice

Copyright © 2020 by Harlequin Books S.A.

This edition published by arrangement with Harlequin Books S.A.

For questions and comments about the quality of this book, please contact us at CustomerService@Harlequin.com.

Love Inspired
22 Adelaide St. West, 40th Floor
Toronto, Ontario M5H 4E3, Canada
www.Harlequin.com

Printed in U.S.A.

It is joy to the just to do judgment:
but destruction shall be to the workers of iniquity.
—Proverbs 21:15

To the wonderful authors who wrote the books
before this one. You are rock stars, and I love you all.

And to Melissa Senate, a woman I have never met, but who
edited this manuscript and helped me add in all the details
that tied it to every continuity book that came before it.
Melissa, from the bottom of my heart, thank you.

ONE

Sasha Eastman had never been afraid to stand on a crowded street corner in Sheepshead Bay, New York. She'd waited at crosswalks hundreds of times, standing amid throngs of people all staring at phones or streetlights and then flowing like lemmings across the roads. She knew the ebb of city life—the busy, noisy, thriving world of people and vehicles and emergency sirens. Since her father's death two years ago, she found the crowds comforting. Each morning she walked out of her quiet apartment and reminded herself that she wasn't alone, that there was a city filled with people surrounding her. She didn't need more than that. She didn't want more. She liked being free of the emotional entanglement relationships brought—the highs and lows, joys and heartbreaks. She'd lost her mother at fourteen years old, lost her ex-husband to another woman after three years of marriage. She'd lost her father to cancer, and she had no intention of losing anyone ever again. Being alone was fine. It was good. She was happy with her two-bedroom apartment and the silence she returned to after a long day of work. She had always felt safe and content in the life she had created.

And then *he'd* appeared.

First, just at the edge of her periphery—a quick glimpse that had made her blood run cold. The hooked nose, the hooded eyes, the stature that was just tall enough to make him stand out in a crowd. She'd told herself she was overtired, working too hard, thinking too much about the past. Martin Roker had died in a gun battle with the police eighteen years ago, shortly after he had murdered Sasha's mother. He was *not* wandering the streets of New York

City. He wasn't stalking her. He wouldn't jump out of her closet in the dead of night.

And yet she hadn't been able to shake the anxiety that settled in the pit of her stomach.

She had seen him again a day later. Full-on face view of a man who should be dead. He'd been standing across the street from the small studio where she taped her show for the local-access cable station, WBKN. She'd walked outside at dusk, ready to return home after a few hours of working on her story. The one she was finally ready to tell: the tragedy of losing a family member to murder and the triumph that could come from it. Her mind had been in the past, her thoughts dwelling on those minutes and hours after she had learned of her mother's death. She'd been looking at her phone, wondering if she should visit the police precinct to ask for the case file on her mother's murder. When she looked up, he had been across the street.

And now...

Now she was afraid in a way she

couldn't remember ever being before. Afraid that she would see him again; worried that delving into past heartaches had unhinged her mind and made her vulnerable to imagining things that couldn't possibly exist.

Like a dead man walking the streets.

She hitched her bag higher on her shoulder, determined to push the fear away. Martin Roker was dead. He had died eighteen years ago—a forty-year-old man who had forced the police to shoot him. He couldn't possibly be stalking her. Even if he had lived, even if he had decided to hunt her down for some twisted reason, he wouldn't still look like a forty-year-old man. He would have aged.

Her cell phone rang and she glanced down, dismissing the number as a solicitor's. When she looked up again, the light had changed and the crowd was moving. She stepped off the curb, scanning the area, her heart jumping as she met cold blue eyes.

He was there! Right in her path, looking

into her eyes as if he were daring her to come closer. Hooked nose. Blondish hair. Taller by a couple of inches than the people around him.

She turned away, heart in her throat, pulse racing. She glanced back, sure that he would be gone. He was crossing the street with long, determined strides, his cold gaze focused on Sasha. Hands deep in the pockets of his coat, shoulders squared, he moved through the crowd without breaking eye contact. Terrified, she ran back the way she had come, dodging the throng of people returning home after work. The studio was three blocks away. She'd go there and call for a cab, because she couldn't call the police and say a dead man was stalking her.

Could she?

She glanced back again, hoping he had been a figment of her imagination and that maybe she was simply exhausted from too many nights thinking about the past and her mother's murder.

He was still there! Moving quickly and gaining on her.

This was real!

He was real!

She ducked into a corner bakery, smiling at the man behind the counter as she ran to the display case and pretended to look at the pastries.

"Can I help you?" he asked.

"Just looking," she murmured, her mouth dry with fear, the smile still pasted on her face. She knew how to fake happiness. She knew how to pretend everything was okay. She'd done it after her mother's murder because she hadn't wanted her father to worry. She'd done it after her ex-husband, Michael, had told her he was in love with another woman, packed his bags and walked out of their apartment. She'd put on her smiles and she had faked her happiness. She was ready to be more authentic. She wanted to be.

She wanted to tell her story and share her experiences. She wanted to hunt for the good in New York City's crowded streets and boroughs and give people something to smile about.

Had her determination to do that caused the past to be resurrected?

She could think of no other reason for a man who looked exactly like her mother's killer to be stalking her. The producer of the local cable news show she worked for had insisted she tell viewers about the two-day special report she was working on. The story of her mother's murder and the aftermath of it. After all these years, Sasha was eager to let the world know that her mother had been a wonderful woman who had made a terrible mistake. A mistake that had cost her life. Following that tragedy, Sasha had become determined to fulfill the dream she had spent so many hours talking to her mother about. Even at a young age, she had known she wanted to be a journalist. Telling her story was part of that.

But had it put her in the crosshairs of a madman?

She shuddered, still staring into the case

and wishing she didn't have to walk outside alone.

The door opened behind her, the quiet whoosh making her skin crawl. She didn't dare turn around. She was too afraid of what she would see. Her shoulders tensed as someone walked across the tile floor.

"Hey, Bradley! You're in early tonight. You want the usual?" the man behind the counter called out cheerfully.

He obviously wasn't seeing a ghoulish monster.

Sasha moved to the side and let her gaze drift to the figure that was stepping up to the counter. Suit. Button-down shirt. Shiny leather shoes. A dog on a leash standing calmly beside him, its dark brown eyes focused on Sasha.

She nearly sagged with relief.

She knew the dog, and she knew the police officer. Detective Bradley McGregor's parents had been murdered in their home twenty years ago. Their four-year-old daughter, Penelope, had been left unhurt. Their fourteen-year-old son, Bradley, out on a sleepover at a friend's apartment, had been the prime suspect. The double homicide had been a hot topic on the local news channels back then. Recently, it had become one again. Earlier this year, a copycat killer had murdered a couple, leaving their young daughter as the only witness. The similarities between the cases had been obvious enough to make people talk.

Sasha had listened.

She'd been young at the time of the McGregor murders, and the details had been blurry. After doing some research and realizing that stories of Bradley's guilt had still circulated for decades after he had been taken off the suspect list, she had known she wanted to interview him for her show.

A local son raised by neglectful parents and suspected of their brutal murders becomes a well-respected K-9 police detective.

What wasn't feel-good about that?

Last week, she'd visited Detective Mc-

Gregor at the precinct, hoping he'd agree to an interview. She'd tried to talk to his sister, Penny, but the young woman, who was the front desk clerk at the Brooklyn K-9 Unit, had said *No comment* at least five times.

Sasha hadn't given up.

She would return to the precinct and ask again, but now wasn't the right time to try to talk Bradley McGregor into an interview. Not when he was watching her tensely, obviously braced for an onslaught of questions and requests.

"Detective," she murmured, refusing to allow his lack of warmth to send her rushing from the bakery. Right now, this was her safe spot. She would hang around until McGregor left. Then she would walk outside with him.

"Ms. Eastman," he responded, his gaze shifting to the man behind the counter. "I'll take my usual, Jack. Throw in a couple of éclairs for my sister."

"Won't be long, she'll be moving out,

hey?" the man said. "Heard she's getting married."

"You heard right."

"Can't believe the little kid you used to bring in for muffins and juice is old enough to fly the coop." He shook his head, his attention jumping to a point beyond Sasha.

He frowned.

"You got trouble, young lady?" he asked.

Startled, she turned and saw her worst nightmare staring in the storefront window. His cold eyes and dead expression were too familiar, his smile chilling as he pulled his hand from his pocket and pointed a gun in her direction.

She screamed, bumping Detective McGregor as she tried to duck away. The crack of gunfire echoed through the bakery, the window exploding into a million tiny fissures that crawled across the glass.

Detective McGregor shouted for her to get down, but she was already on the floor, scrambling for cover behind the counter. The door opened and closed, and

she had no idea if McGregor had run outside or if Martin Roker had entered. She
cowered behind the counter and waited as
the sounds of sirens and people shouting
drifted in from the street.

Detective Bradley McGregor raced
down the crowded sidewalk, dodging pedestrians as he shouted for the gunman
to stop. His Belgian Malinois partner,
King, trained for protection but excellent at tracking and at suspect apprehension, loped beside him. Head up and ears
pricked, King was waiting to be issued the
command to attack. If the streets had been
empty, if there weren't dozens of people
around, Bradley would have already given
it. The perp was a half block ahead, dark
coat flapping like bat wings as he sprinted
past stunned onlookers. He had tucked his
gun away or tossed it. Both his hands were
free. Bradley could see the paleness of his
skin and the long, thin length of his legs.
Dark slacks. Black coat. Short blond hair.
Armed.

Dangerous.

He called for backup, his radio buzzing with life as officers responded. He could count on his team to be there swiftly, but he wanted the perp off the streets now, before anyone was hurt.

"Police! Freeze!" he yelled as he dodged a woman with a baby in a carrier who was desperately looking for an escape route. People were panicking, short high-pitched screams and anxious shouts creating a cacophony of noise that rivaled the normal raucous sounds of rush hour in the city.

The perp veered to the right, sprinting into one of the narrow alleys that opened between buildings. This was where things got dicey. No visual of the perp. No way of knowing if he was running or preparing an ambush. They were near Ocean Avenue, the busy thoroughfare surrounded by newer multifamily dwellings. Closer to the bay, older homes dotted the quieter streets.

He slowed as he reached the alley, staying close to the brick facade of an apartment building as he called in his location. Whoever this guy was, whomever his target had been, he needed to be stopped.

"Police! Come out or I'm sending my dog in." He gave one last warning as he unhooked King's leash. The Malinois was a mild-mannered, high-energy pet at home, but he became a fierce weapon out in the field.

King snarled, teeth bared, body tense. His scruff was up, his ears back. He was ready.

"Hold on, Officer. I'm coming!" a man yelled out from the alley.

"Slowly! Hands where I can see them!" Bradley responded, keeping hold of King's collar. The dog was scrabbling at the pavement, barking wildly. King loved anything to do with his job, but this part of the game? When he was let loose to do what he had been trained to do? It was his favorite.

"I'm coming, man! Hold the dog!" Someone shuffled into view. A man in his fifties or sixties. Scruffy gray beard and pallid skin. Dark blue sweatpants that hadn't been washed in a while. Oversize coat hanging from a too-thin frame. Not the perp. This guy had just been in the wrong place at the wrong time.

"Step to the side," Bradley commanded. "You see a guy run through that alley?"

"Tall dude? Blond hair? Yeah. He ran past me. I said hello, but he didn't give me the time of day otherwise," the man said, his focus on King, his dark blue eyes wide with fear. "You're not letting him go, are you?"

"No." Bradley's response was terse, his focus on the alley again. The perp was heading toward Sheepshead Bay and deeper into the quietest areas of the community. 1920s houses converted to apartments. Single-family homes on small lots that abutted one another. A nice residential community in Brooklyn, Sheepshead Bay wasn't known for its high crime rate. Once a fishing town, it offered a more suburban feel for city dwellers who wanted it.

It also offered plenty of escape routes.

He hooked King back to his leash and ran through the alley, bursting out onto the next street as the sun ducked behind rows of brick apartment buildings. There was a chill of winter in the air that blew in from the bay, hinting at the holiday season that would soon envelop the city. Bradley dreaded it the same way other people dreaded trips to the dentist.

Thanksgiving first. The holiday where families and friends gathered to give thanks for their blessings and for each other. Then Christmas, where the same thing played out. It wasn't that Bradley didn't enjoy gathering with people he cared about, but holidays were a reminder of what life could have and should have been. He and Penny growing up in a loving home with loving parents. No murder to taint their memories. No need for a loving adoptive family to take them in.

There had been blessings that had come out of the pain, but Bradley couldn't help wondering if there had been a purpose behind the struggles and trials. He had certainly learned a lot about life and about himself, but he had also had to work hard to overcome his rough beginning.

Aside from valuing what he had, loving deeply the people in his life, mostly he had learned to protect himself by building an impeccable reputation in the community.

Even that hadn't been enough.

He had heard the whispers after a copy-cat murder had rocked the community—a husband and wife killed, their three-year-old daughter the only witness. Even after all these years, after all he had accomplished in his work as a police officer, people had still wondered if he was responsible for his parents' murders.

Now that the perpetrator had been caught, there was no doubt of his innocence. The whispers had stopped, but the sting of them hadn't left him. He loved New York City. He loved Brooklyn and Sheepshead Bay. He had served the people of the city faithfully for more than a decade.

And still they had doubted him.

He frowned, scanning the street, and spotted the perp dashing across the pavement, his black coat flapping behind him. There were still too many people to safely release King. Protection-and-apprehension dogs were trained to take down the threat. They were not trained to differentiate the scent of the threat from the surrounding population. A straight and clear path between the dog and the suspect was necessary for safe deployment.

Right now, Bradley didn't have it.

He called in his location again as he sprinted across the street, dodging a bicyclist and several motorists who were surprised to see a police officer and dog darting through evening traffic.

Bradley knew the area well. The suspect ran through a packed parking lot, jumped a small retaining wall and kept going, ducking into a parking garage connected to one of the newer apartment complexes. He followed, moving more cautiously as he stepped into the dimly lit interior. There were too many turns and angles, too many cars, too many places where the gunman could be lying in wait. He kept a wall to his left shoulder and King to his right as he scanned the area. No sign of the gunman. No sounds of him fleeing. Bradley gave King the command to find and let the dog lead him through a maze of parked cars. There was a stairwell in the far wall, and King lunged into it, straining against the leash and barking wildly.

"Police! Come out with your hands where I can see them," Bradley commanded.

There was a flurry of movement on the landing above. A door opened and slammed closed, and King scrabbled at the cement steps.

"Let's go!" Bradley raced up the stairs, slamming his hand into the closed door and rushing out onto the third level of the parking garage. A car engine revved as he and King sprinted across the paved lot. King swung around, barking wildly as tires squealed and a small blue car sped around a corner and aimed straight for them.

Bradley shouted for the vehicle to halt, then pulled his service weapon, firing at the front tire of the vehicle as he dived for cover.

TWO

Martin Roker was alive.

He had been outside the bakery.

He had fired a shot through the window.

Sasha hadn't gone crazy.

She wasn't imagining things.

Her sleepless nights and long hours of work weren't making her hallucinate.

She frowned.

She had seen Martin three times in a week. Each time, she'd been convinced he was an unaged version of the man who had murdered her mother. Forty years old. Tall and angular. No wrinkles visible on his thin face.

"Impossible," she whispered as she watched several police officers collect evidence outside the bakery. When they'd arrived, she had been asked to have a seat and wait. Forty minutes later, and she was still waiting. The sky had turned navy with twilight, the city lights flickering on. Cars inched by the police barrier that had been erected at the curb, blue and white lights flashing on windows and pavement.

The man who had been stalking her had caused all this.

Martin Roker?

It couldn't be. Not an unaged, unchanged man in a world where everything aged and everything changed. Eighteen years was a long time. If Roker had lived, he would be close to sixty, with some gray hair and at least a few wrinkles. He'd have changed the way everyone did. Life left no one unscathed.

"He's dead," she muttered, reminding herself of the most important fact.

Martin Roker had been killed in a shootout with the police. Recently, she had looked through the files and the evidence that had been collected after her mother's murder. She had seen photos of Roker's body, lying where it had fallen, the area cordoned off by yellow police tape. She had felt for the wife and little girl he had left behind, and she had considered contacting them for her story.

She hadn't wanted to dredge up a past that she knew had been as painful for them as it had been for her. They were not responsible for Roker's actions, and their suffering in the aftermath only made his affair with Sasha's mother, the murder and his suicide-by-police all the more heartbreaking.

She had left them alone.

Despite her journalistic need for all the facts and all sides of the story, she had shut herself off from that part of the past.

But now she wondered if she had been wrong to do so.

Roker couldn't be stalking her through the streets of Sheepshead Bay. He couldn't have fired a gun at her.

But someone was. Someone had.

Who?

She needed to know. The only way she

was going to find out was to dig into Roker's side of the story. Look into the life he had lived before he had murdered her mother.

Somewhere in the past was a clue about the present. She just had to find it.

"Are you okay?" the bakery attendant asked, plopping a bottle of water on the table in front of her before she could respond. "You look pale."

"It comes with the blond hair," she responded, offering a shaky smile.

"More likely comes from being shot at."

"That, too," she murmured, opening the bottle and taking a sip. Her hands were shaking and water sloshed onto her coat and the table.

"Who is he? An ex?"

"Ex?" She swiped at the drops of water, flicking them from the table before she dropped into a chair. She didn't consider herself to be easily scared, and she certainly wouldn't label herself as someone who got overly excited in chaotic situations. She tended to be the calm in the storm, the person people turned to when they needed a clear mind and a focused approach.

Right now, though, she was shaken.

Deeply.

"Ex," the man responded, pulling out a chair and sitting across from her. "Husband? Boyfriend?"

"Oh. No. It isn't anyone I know," she replied, glancing at the activity outside the window. What evidence were they collecting? What were they looking for? Shell casings? Bullets? Some clue that would give them a name and location for the perp? "Do you have security cameras outside?" she asked, falling back into old habits from her days as a newspaper reporter working the crime beat. That had been her first job. She'd learned a lot about law enforcement and the criminal justice system during those five years.

She'd also gotten burned out.

Too many hard-luck stories.

Too many atrocities committed against humans by humans.

She'd spent a lot of time praying back then, a lot of time writing in her journal, listing people who desperately needed answers or closure or healing. She had wanted to help all of them, and she had wanted to understand what caused a person to hurt someone else.

She hadn't been able to do either of those things.

In the end, she had walked away rather than become jaded and cynical. She hadn't wanted the job to change her.

"I'm afraid we don't. Place is too old-fashioned for that."

"Old-fashioned? It looks nicely updated," she responded absently, years of interviewing people making the conversation almost rote.

"Oh. It is. We keep up with the times, but I never felt the need for anything more than a lock on the front and back doors. People in the neighborhood know my shop, know me. Why would they want to do anything to hurt what my family built?"

"They wouldn't, and there are plenty of other businesses on the street. I'm sure some of them have security cameras." She took another sip of water. Her hand was steadier, but her heart was still beating rapidly, her pulse racing.

The man couldn't have been Martin Roker.

So, who was he?

Why had he been following her?

Why had he fired a shot at her?

"True, but I'll still be getting a security system and camera in the next few days. Not going to have riffraff causing problems around the bakery. We've worked too hard to keep this place going."

"I'm really sorry this happened."

"It's not your fault." He smiled jovially and stood. "I'm going to the kitchen. Probably won't be able to open tomorrow. Might as well clean up and get ready to end the day."

He walked into the back of the store.

She stayed where she was, facing the window and the lights, the dark evening sky and the familiar street. She had made Sheepshead Bay her home a decade ago, moving into an apartment that was within walking distance of the subway station. She'd just graduated from college, was newly married and searching for a job in journalism. Life had been exciting and filled with possibilities.

Ten years later, she had achieved some of her dreams. She had reached for others only to see them slip through her fingers. She had lost her father to cancer. She had lost her marriage to infidelity. She was still in the apartment and still working in journalism, but her focus had changed.

She didn't want to change the world so much as she wanted to cheer it. She couldn't take away pain or heartache, but she could put positive stories out into the world.

Or at least in the small area of the world her cable show reached.

She didn't reach for big dreams.

Not anymore.

She prayed for small successes. That

God would use her to touch a heart, to ease a burden, to lift a spirt—those were the things she wanted. She had thought she was making progress toward that. Her life had fallen into a nice routine. Early-morning walk to work. A few hours of prep. Produce a live cable show that high-lighted the good things that were happening in the community. A late lunch. A few more hours of work. An early-evening walk through Sheepshead Bay, enjoying the cacophony of city noise and the frenetic pace of life.

And then Martin Roker had appeared.

First outside her apartment at twilight, standing across the street as she walked home. The light had been dim. She had told herself she was mistaken, that it wasn't him, but her stomach had churned with anxiety.

She had dreamed about her mother that night, waking bathed in sweat with her heart tripping and jumping, terrified and not sure why.

She pushed away from the table, tired

of her circling thoughts and her dead-end reasoning. She knew what she had seen. There was no doubt about it. What she needed to find out was who the Martin Roker look-alike was.

She stepped outside, smiling at a female police officer who was standing on the sidewalk a few feet away.

"I'm not trying to rush the process, but I was wondering how long I'm going to have to wait to be interviewed," she said.

"We're finishing up. If you'll go inside and wait a little longer, we should be with you shortly," the female officer said. She had green eyes and a kind smile. Sasha guessed her to be in her early twenties. Probably new to police work.

"Have you heard anything from Detective McGregor?" she asked, ignoring the subtle request to leave.

"I'm not that high up on the food chain," the officer responded.

"Is there someone here who is?"

"My sergeant. He's next to his cruiser." She pointed to the corner of the street and three uniformed officers who were standing at the curb.

"Thank you." Sasha skirted crime scene tape, her energy amping up, her nerves simmering down. Action was better than idleness. That had been her father's mantra after her mother died. Keep going. Keep moving forward. Keep the mind and the body occupied so the grief doesn't win.

"Ms. Eastman!" a man called.

She swung around and was surprised to see Detective McGregor striding toward her, his canine partner at his side. The dog seemed relaxed, tongue lolling out, bright eyes focused on Sasha.

McGregor, on the other hand, looked unhappy, his jaw tight, his expression grim.

"Were you leaving?" he asked.

"I was looking for you. Any success catching the gunman?" she asked, certain from the expression on his face he hadn't had any.

"How about we go inside to discuss it?"

"That's fine." She followed him into the

bakery, staying a few feet away from his Malinois. Aside from what she had seen on television, she knew nothing about police dogs and how they worked.

"Don't worry," Detective McGregor said as he pulled out a chair and motioned for her to sit. "King doesn't bite unless he's told to."

"I wasn't worried."

"No?" He took the seat across from her and stared into her eyes. She resisted the urge to look away. Face-to-face interviews were her thing. She knew how to meet eyes and make polite conversation, but she felt off-balance as she met McGregor's gaze. He was different from other police officers she'd interviewed.

Or maybe she just perceived him that way because she knew his background and because she understood how difficult it was to break away from the past. She admired him for his success. Professionally and personally. To have had such a rough beginning and to have created good things from that was something she was interested in exploring in her work.

"I don't know much about police dogs, but I'm not afraid of them. Much," she admitted, watching as King settled down beside Bradley.

Bradley laughed. "A little caution around a dog like King isn't a bad thing. He is trained in protection and apprehension. A powerful tool and a very good partner. Unfortunately, we couldn't catch the gunman. We tracked him to an apartment parking garage. He had a vehicle there, and he was able to escape." He didn't look away as he spoke. His eyes were the darkest brown she had ever seen, his hair a rich chestnut with hints of auburn. She hadn't noticed that when she'd gone to the precinct to ask for an interview, and she probably shouldn't be noticing now.

"Did you get a look at his vehicle?" she asked, following the same line of questioning she would have used if she had still been working the crime beat. She needed answers. Bradley might have them.

"Yes. We're also getting security footage from apartment management. It may take a little time, so I wanted to fill you in and let you know—we're working as fast and as diligently as we can."

"I appreciate that, Detective."

"I'm sure you'll also understand and appreciate the fact that I have some questions I'd like to ask. If you're up to it."

"I am." She pulled her coat a little tighter, cold with the thought that the man who looked like Martin Roker was still free. She had been hopeful he would be caught. That this would be over as quickly as it had begun. She had work to do, feel-good stories to tell.

And her own past to explore.

With Thanksgiving coming up, it had seemed as good a time as any to explore her heritage. Her grandparents had been gone for years. She had no aunts or uncles. No family members who might remember her parents as children. She had been contacting old friends of her parents, interviewing teachers who remembered them, trying to put together the beginning of the story that had become hers.

She didn't want to be here, the victim of a crime.

She wanted to be figuring out her past so that maybe she could begin planning a future that involved more than going to work in the morning and returning to her empty apartment each night.

"So, let's get started," he said, taking out a small notebook and a pen. "Did you get a good look at the perpetrator?"

"Yes."

"Good enough to pick him out of a lineup?" he asked, jotting her answers down.

"Absolutely."

"Did you recognize him?"

"Yes."

He stopped writing and met her eyes.

"Want to tell me who he is?"

"I can tell you who he looks like."

"Okay, how about you do that?" he said, a hint of impatience in his voice.

"He looks just like the man who murdered my mother."

He set the pen on the table, crossed his arms over his chest, his dark eyes spearing into hers. "Let's back up. Your mother was murdered?"

"Yes."

"Recently?"

"No," she said, offering a quick, emotionless account of what had happened.

When she finished, he nodded. "I think I remember hearing about the case. The murderer was killed by the police."

"That's right."

"And yet you think he was here tonight? Firing a gun?"

"I think someone who looks exactly like him was."

He frowned. "Why?"

"Why do I think that? Or why would the dead ringer for my mother's killer stalk me?"

"Stalk you?"

"I've seen him twice before today," she explained.

"What's the name of the man who killed your mother?" he asked. To his credit, he didn't voice doubts, didn't tell her she was imagining things or ask if she might be mistaken.

"Martin Roker."

He nodded. "All right. Wait here. I want to make a few calls, and then we'll talk more."

He told King to stay, walked outside and stood near the door, cell phone pressed to his ear, gaze still focused on Sasha. She knew he thought she was delusional. She would think the same if she'd heard the cockamamie story she had just told.

She stood, restless and uneasy.

King growled, the sound just enough of a warning to make her drop into the chair again. She wasn't afraid of the dog, but she wasn't willing to take chances around him, either. She would wait. Maybe Mc-Gregor would return with information that would make everything she had experienced make sense.

* * *

A dead man stalking and shooting at Sasha Eastman?

It wasn't possible.

She seemed very aware of that fact. Yet she had still told him that the shooter was a dead ringer for her mother's murderer.

Bradley kept his attention focused on her as he called the precinct and asked for information on Martin Roker. It only took a few minutes for a clerk in the records office to confirm that Roker had murdered his ex-love, Natasha Eastman, and was killed in a shoot-out with the police.

The evening had taken a confusing turn, but there was one thing he was certain of—dead men did not fire guns.

On the other hand, Sasha didn't seem like the kind of person who was given to imagining things. After she had visited him at the precinct, he had made it a point to watch her cable show. He'd been curious and then pleasantly surprised by the upbeat, hope-filled stories she presented to viewers. He would never have guessed that she had been through the tragedy of losing a parent to violence.

But then, most people wouldn't guess that about him.

Not that anyone in Sheepshead Bay would need to guess. Anyone who had been in the community for any length of time knew the story of his parents' murders. A man, wearing a clown mask with blue hair, had broken into his parents' home. He'd shot Anna and Eddie McGregor but hadn't hurt their daughter, Penny. She had only been four at the time. Instead of harming her, the perpetrator had given her a stuffed monkey. Both unemployed at the time of the murders, Bradley's parents had been small-time criminals who liked to go out and party. They had been neglectful regarding the well-being of their kids. By the time of their murders, Bradley had been fourteen and well used to his parents' selfishness and indifference. He hadn't cared about it for himself, but he had been angry that Penny was often left alone with no food while he was at school. When his parents had the money to bring her to day care, they often forgot to pick her up at the end of the day.

Bradley had been determined to make certain Penny didn't suffer, he had been angry at his parents, he had wanted them to do better, but he had loved them. That he'd been considered a suspect in their murders, even briefly, had hurt. Worse, he'd been the prime suspect for just long enough to cement the community's distrust and suspicion of him, even twenty years later. The case had gone cold and would have been long forgotten if a copycat killer hadn't struck on the twentieth anniversary of the killings. Another couple, also neglectful of their young daughter, was murdered in their Brooklyn home. Little Lucy Emery had been left unhurt and given a stuffed monkey.

Same MO.

Different killer.

He knew that for a fact, because the perpetrator of the Emery murders was still on the loose.

His parents' murderer, finally identified through DNA, was now rotting in prison, awaiting trial.

Bradley was very much looking forward to seeing Randall Gage face justice. For his parents. For Penny.

For him.

Sometimes he still felt like that four-teen-year-old kid being interrogated and watched. It had hurt to have people he admired and trusted whisper when he walked by. It had been painful to realize that they could so easily begin to question his honesty and integrity. He'd spent the past twenty years proving who he was to the community. His parents may have been low-level criminals, but that didn't mean he had to follow in their footsteps. Thankfully for him and Penny, the detective on his parents' case and his wife had taken them in, giving them stability, room to grieve, to be confused. Bradley had taken the hard road—college, career, helping raise his younger sister. He had no regrets, but he had never forgotten the sting of being suspected of a heinous crime. He thought about it every time he worked a case. He never wanted to be responsible for tainting a person's reputation without cause, and he certainly wasn't going to treat Sasha like she had lost her mind because of her allegations.

The shooter had been very much alive. Bradley had gotten a good look at him. He planned to return to the precinct and search for photos of Martin Roker. It had been eighteen years since his death and since Sasha had seen him. It was possible the shooter looked similar enough to confuse her.

He walked back into the bakery and called King to heel.

"I verified Roker's death," he said as Sasha approached.

"I already knew he was dead. What I'd like to figure out is how a dead man could possibly be stalking me through the streets of Sheepshead Bay." She had a direct gaze and a straightforward approach to communication that he appreciated.

"You of course know that isn't possible."

"I do. I also know what I've seen. The man who is stalking me is Martin Roker's doppelgänger."

"I'll do everything I can to figure out who he is. Until I do, it's probably best if you stay close to home. Keep your doors locked. Don't go out alone."

"I have a job, Detective. I can't just blow it off."

"Your life is more important than your job, Ms. Eastman."

"I'll be careful, but I can't spend an indefinite amount of time locked in my apartment. Speaking of which—" she glanced at her watch and frowned "—do you think I'll be allowed to go home any time tonight?"

"I just need your contact information, and then you're free to go."

She rattled it off, then handed him a business card. "It's all here."

"Thanks. I'll keep you updated on our progress."

"I appreciate it, Detective." She walked to the door, her expression cool. Her hand shook as she tucked a stray strand of hair behind her ear. She wasn't nearly as unaffected as she pretended to be.

And he wasn't going to be able to let her walk away knowing that she was terrified.

"How about King and I escort you home?" he suggested, following her out into the cold November evening.

"I'd tell you that isn't necessary, but I'm a little shaken by what happened. I'd appreciate the escort," she responded.

"You said you've seen the gunman before?" he asked, moving so that he and King were positioned between Sasha and the street.

"I saw him as I was leaving work one day and then again when I was walking home a few days later."

"And you thought it was the man who murdered your mother?"

"I didn't think it was him. Not really.

Roker would be close to sixty. The man I saw was more like forty. The same age Roker was when he murdered my mother." She shuddered.

"A family member maybe," he commented, wondering if Martin Roker had a twin who might have had a son.

"I suppose so."

"You don't sound convinced."

"The resemblance was uncanny, but..." She shrugged.

"But what?"

"I don't believe in ghosts, Detective. Obviously, if Martin Roker died, he couldn't be stalking me through the streets of New York City." They turned a corner onto a quiet residential street lined with stately brownstones that had once been summer homes for the wealthy. Now they were apartments rented by young professionals and growing families.

"It's possible he had a twin. Or a sibling."

"He was an only child. Raised by a single mother. If he had biological siblings, they'd have been on his father's side. Based on the research I've done, I doubt they would have known him well enough to want revenge for his death."

"Research?" he asked as she pulled keys from her bag and hurried up the cement stairs of one of the brownstones. The four-story house had once been a stately single-family dwelling. Now it was split into several apartment units.

"I'm telling my mother's story on the cable program I host. I was a teenager when she was killed, and a lot of the details are hazy. I guess I put them out of my head." She punched in the code and ushered him into a narrow stairway. "My unit is on the second floor. You don't have to accompany me. I'll be fine from here."

"I like to finish what I start," he responded, following her up a flight of stairs to the second-floor landing.

"Me, too." She unlocked the only door on the second level and stepped inside, hanging her bag from a hook near the door and slipping out of her coat.

"Would you like coffee? Soda? Water?" she asked, draping the coat across the back of a bright yellow chair.

"Water. If you don't mind," he responded. He wasn't thirsty, but he did want to spend a few more minutes in the apartment. Get a better feel for its security strengths and weaknesses.

"For you and the dog?" she asked with a smile that softened her face and made her look a decade younger than he'd imagined her to be.

"King would probably appreciate that."

"King? I thought maybe his name was Cujo." She stepped into the galley-style kitchen. The living area and kitchen flowed together, all of it decorated in grays and yellows.

"I tried to name him that, but my supervisor refused to allow it," he said, crossing the room and looking out one of the large windows. Not much of a view, but a fire escape jutted out from the window.

"Did you really?" she asked, filling a

plastic bowl with water and setting it on the floor.

"What do you think?" He checked the window lock. Sturdy but not unbreakable.

"You're much too serious to make a joke out of your partner's name."

Surprised, he turned to look at her. "Why do you say that?"

"Am I wrong?" She grabbed two bottles of water from the refrigerator and handed him one.

"Probably not."

"You don't know?"

"I suppose how serious I am depends on the situation." He dropped King's lead and watched as he trotted to the bowl and lapped up water like he hadn't had a drink in months. "I'm very serious about my job."

"I got that impression when I visited you at the precinct," she said, glancing out the window and frowning. "Are you looking for something?"

"Easy access points. Weak locks. Ways

that someone might be able to get into the apartment."

"I keep the windows locked."

"How about in the bedrooms?"

She frowned. "To be honest, I've never thought about it. I'm two floors up. A person would need a ladder to get to the windows, and I can't imagine anyone being bold enough to put a ladder up and break in."

"Someone was bold enough to fire shots into a bakery where a police officer was standing," he pointed out.

"Point taken."

"So, how about we check those windows before I leave?" he suggested.

"Sure. Why not?" She led him into a short hallway. Two doors on one wall. One door on the other. She opened one, motioning him to follow.

The room was small. Maybe ten by ten. One window. A closet opened to reveal a file cabinet and shelves lined with boxes. A secretary desk stood against one wall, papers strewn across its surface, a stack of newspapers beside it. "Excuse the mess. I'm juggling a few different projects. Lots of research."

"For your cable show?"

"Yes."

She walked to the lone window, opened the shades and checked the lock. "This one is secure. There's a sliding glass door in my room. It opens to a balcony."

"Can I take a look?" he asked.

"I'm confident in my ability to know a locked door from an unlocked one, but if it'll make you feel better, you can." She sidled past him and hurried into the hall.

He was surprised by her rush to get rid of him. She wanted a story from him. *The* story from him. The one about his parents' murders, about the way it had felt to be a suspect in their deaths, about the years since then. The hard work he had put into building his reputation as a good police officer and a trustworthy person. He had no intention of sharing that with the world. He rarely shared it with friends. Even his sister, Penny, had no real idea of how much those few days of suspicion had cost, how difficult it had been for Bradley to face friends and family who had—even if only for a moment—wondered if he had killed his parents. He'd been cleared not long after the murders, but he'd had to wait twenty years for the killer to be identified and caught. Everyone was relieved that Randall Gage was in prison awaiting trial, but for Bradley, the echo of those long-ago accusations still rang loudly in his mind.

He followed Sasha into a room that was smaller than the office. A double bed took up most of the space. A narrow dresser stood between it and the wall. Six drawers. A lamp sitting on top, a framed photo beside it. He glanced at it as he walked by. An old church. Sasha in a wedding dress. An older man in a dark suit standing with his arm around her.

"Your wedding?" he asked, touching the white frame.

"What gave it away? The fancy hairdo?

The church? The wedding dress?" She added the last with a quick smile.

"My keen powers of detection," he responded.

She laughed. "You do have a sense of humor!"

"You're surprised?"

"Maybe." She pulled back bright blue curtains and gestured to a sliding glass door. "It's locked."

"You might want more than a lock," he said, opening the door and stepping onto the balcony. King followed, nudged close to his leg, his rangy body relaxed. He didn't mind balconies, escalators, elevators. He'd been trained indoors and out, run through courses in a variety of situations designed to test his environmental tolerance and confidence. Like other K-9s, King had excelled during training and in his work.

The balcony was three feet wide and six feet long. A gate on one end opened to stairs that led to a small patch of grass at the side of the house. From where he stood, Bradley could see a corner of the street and a portion of the neighboring yard. "This would make an easy access point if someone wanted to gain entrance," he said, opening the gate and stepping onto the wrought steps. They clanged under his weight. "Have you considered a security system?"

"No, but it's probably a good idea," she responded, her gaze shifting from Bradley to the yard. "I don't spend much time on the balcony. Especially not lately."

"Too chilly?" he asked, probing the darkness just beyond the yard. Several trash cans sat near the neighbor's fence. Nothing alarming about that, but he was on edge and antsy.

"Too exposed," she replied.

"You've been nervous lately?" He grabbed her arm, tugging her back to the door.

"Wouldn't you be, if someone who looked like your mother's murderer was stalking you?"

"Yes," he conceded. He had spent two

decades wondering if his parents' killer was somewhere close by. That had made him pay attention to his surroundings and study the people around him. He wouldn't say he had been jumpy, but he had certainly been very aware of the possibility that danger could be close by.

King growled, his scruff suddenly up, his body stiff. Ears pressed close to his head, tail high and taut, amber eyes focused on the tiny sliver of street.

He sensed something.

Bradley gave Sasha a gentle shove into the house. "Close the door. Lock it. Stay away from the windows."

"What's going on?"

"Close the door and lock it," he repeated.

She frowned but did as he asked, sliding the door closed, snapping the lock down. He waited until she had moved away from the glass. When she was gone, he grabbed King's leash and headed down the balcony stairs. The night was quiet, the muted sounds of traffic and city life drifting on the brisk fall breeze.

King's ears perked, his scruff still raised as he sniffed the air. He growled, his attention focused on the house across the street, its yard dotted with large bushes and tall trees.

Someone was there.

King was issuing a warning, and Bradley would be a fool not to heed it.

"Police," he called. "Come on out of there."

No response. Not even a rustle of leaves or whisper of fabric.

"I said, come out!" he called again. "If you refuse, I'll send my dog in." It was a warning he was required to issue. Most criminals responded by surrendering or running. Dogs like King were known to be well trained and vicious when they attacked. There would be no hesitation and no backing down. If King was sent to apprehend a suspect, he got the job done.

Still no response.

Bradley unhooked King's lead, checking the surroundings to be certain no pedestrians were around.

The street was empty, the night settled heavy and dark on the surrounding houses. Long shadows undulated as trees swayed in the November breeze. A few houses still had jack-o'-lanterns and potted chrysanthemums sitting on their stoops. A few cutout cartoon turkeys graced the windows of several homes. The vibe was peaceful, people tucked safely inside, planning the coming month, looking forward to Thanksgiving meals and holiday prep. They had no idea that danger was lurking outside their doors.

"Last chance!" Bradley called. "Come out!"

Nothing.

He released his hold.

King bounded forward, snarling viciously as he sprinted across the street.

THREE

Sasha stood at the sliding glass door, nose nearly touching the glass. The road was visible from her apartment, the well-lit pavement a slash of slate against cement curbs. She'd watched as Detective McGregor and King had raced across the street and out of sight. Had they found her stalker?

Whoever it was hadn't made a secret of the fact that he was hunting Sasha. He had allowed himself to be seen three times. Then he had fired shots into a bakery, not caring that there had been witnesses inside.

"Who would do something like that?" she muttered, walking to the file cabinet that sat beside the antique desk she had inherited from her father. It had been her mother's. Natasha had loved old things. Books. Furniture. Clothes. She'd had a vintage style that had made her the cool mom in Sasha's group of friends.

The cool mom who had cheated on her husband.

Who had nearly wrecked their family.

Who had paid with her life.

Sasha had spent too many years dwelling on what might have been *if only*. Since her father's death, she had done her best to focus on what was and to live with the same grace and forgiveness for her mother that he had always demonstrated. Anders and Natasha had been Russian immigrants. They had arrived in the United States as college students, had met, fallen in love and married. Sasha could still remember the early years of her life, when her parents had seemed so happy and so perfectly suited for one another.

"No one is perfectly suited for anyone," she reminded herself as she opened the top drawer of the file cabinet and pulled a folder out. Filled with information about her mother's murder case, it also contained photos of both her parents when they were kids. She had compiled everything she could, hoping to use it on her show.

Her show?

The cable station's show.

It might be a small-budget program, but she was passionate about her vision for it, her goal. Her boss hadn't been as keen, but Prudence Landry was nothing if not open-minded. She had given Sasha a year to prove that the people of Brooklyn really were desperate for good news. Of course they were. When the Emerys, a young married couple, were murdered in their Brooklyn home months ago, their little girl left an orphan, residents of the borough had been shaken enough. Then to learn it was a copycat killing on the twentieth anniversary of the original double homicide—the murders of the Mc-Gregors, Bradley's parents. With that old case solved, the McGregors' killer in prison, Brooklynites could breathe a collective sigh of relief. But the Emerys' killer was still out there.

Sasha's show felt essential to her.

So far, the ratings were good. People around Brooklyn approached her at the store and on the street to offer feel-good stories about local people doing kind and generous things.

That was what the world needed.

Not the negative, sad and depressing news that network stations often featured. She dropped the folder onto the desk and thumbed through its contents, scanning news articles for information about Roker. Not that she needed a reminder of what the folder contained. She had spent hours poring over it. She knew Roker had been married but separated at the time of the murder. She knew he had left his wife and young daughter in the hopes that he could win Natasha back. When that hadn't worked, he had begun stalking her, showing up at her place of employment, standing in the street light outside their house at night. He had sent cards and letters for months, the tone of them becoming darker and more threatening. Natasha hadn't shown the letters to anyone. They had been found in her dresser after her death.

Sasha had memorized the cold facts of the case.

She hadn't had to try to understand the impact on the victim's family. She had lived it. Telling her story was supposed to be about letting go of the darkest chapter of her life.

She had really thought she could do that. Instead, the past refused to die.

She thumbed through photocopied news articles, found the one with a photo of Martin Roker and shuddered. That was him. The man she had seen on the street.

She pulled it from the pile. Roker and the man who had been stalking her had the same nose. The same light-colored hair. The same cold blue eyes. Was there a difference in the chin? In the tilt of the head?

She studied the photo, her heart thumping painfully. She didn't want to think about Detective McGregor and King chasing an armed man. She wanted to focus on Roker's face and try to prove to herself that he and her stalker were not the same man.

"Of course they aren't. Martin Roker is dead," she muttered, carrying the photo to the balcony. It had been published by a tabloid, his face taking up most of the front page. The article was a long one. More a sensationalized account than a factual one. A Russian immigrant. An affair. A scorned lover. It was all perfect fodder for tabloid news.

"There has to be more personal information about him." She scanned the article, hoping to find a gem of information hidden amid the gossip. Nothing. An estranged wife. One daughter.

At least, Sasha thought she would have.

She jotted a reminder on the pad she kept beside her computer, pulled the sticky note off and stuck it to the mirror above her dresser. There were several other notes there. Her to-do list seemed to get longer every day. Her done list was nonexistent. The last week had been filled with anxiety and constant questions to herself about whether she was losing her mind.

Dead men did not walk the streets.

And yet she had been certain she had been seeing a dead man.

His son.

A brother's son.

None of which he had, according to records. Martin had been an only child, so no identical twin. He also had only one child, a daughter, with his estranged wife. So no look-alike son.

Regardless, she couldn't understand why anyone related to Roker would come after her. She'd been fourteen when her mother died. She hadn't ever met Martin Roker. She hadn't even known about his existence until after the shooting. She had done nothing to call attention to herself or her past.

Yet.

Could someone have found out that she

planned to tell the story on her show? Could that person be trying to stop her?

She jotted another note. A reminder to speak to the detective who had been in charge of the case. He might know if there was anyone who would be impacted if she dredged up the past.

Someone knocked on the door, the sound breaking the silence and sending her pulse racing again.

She hurried to the peephole and looked out into the hall, nearly sagging with relief when she saw Detective McGregor.

She yanked the door open, stepping back so he could enter the apartment. "What happened?" she asked breathlessly.

"He had a car parked at the end of the street," Detective McGregor said, crowding close as King trotted past and settled near the sofa. The dog was panting, his tongue lolling out to the side, his bright brown eyes focused on his partner.

"You saw it?"

"Yes. We almost had him," he growled, his frustration obvious.

"He had a good head start. You can't be too hard on yourself for not catching him."

"Sure I can," he responded, offering a quick smile that took some of the gruffness out of the response. "I radioed in a description of the vehicle. Unfortunately, there was no license plate."

"A stolen vehicle?" she asked.

"Probably. We've issued a BOLO. I don't think it will be long to track it down. I doubt he'll be with it."

"Did you see him?"

"He was tall and thin. Just like the guy who fired the shot into the bakery. I didn't see his face, but if I were into guessing things, I'd guess it was him."

"It's a reasonable guess."

"Maybe. But I like facts. Not speculation."

"After what you went through as a teen, that's not surprising," she said, regretting it immediately. She had done her research. She knew that he had been a suspect in his parents' murders. He had been cleared quickly, but the stain of it, the whispers that had followed him for years, had given him an excuse to be bitter and angry. Instead, he had worked hard. He had devoted himself to law enforcement. He had made a name for himself with the NYPD. She wanted to tell the story. One of overcoming and thriving.

But when she had visited the precinct to ask him for an interview, he'd given her a flat no and walked away.

"I'd rather not discuss my past, Ms. Eastman."

"Sasha," she said. "Everyone calls me that."

He nodded. "You don't have a security system here, and I don't feel comfortable leaving you alone tonight. It would be too easy for someone to break through the sliding glass door."

She wanted to believe no one would be that bold, but after what had happened at the bakery, she couldn't.

"Do you have family you could stay with? A friend? Maybe somewhere outside of Brooklyn? Outside of the city would be even better."

She had plenty of acquaintances, but she had spent the years after her divorce caring for her sick father. What friends she'd had left after the divorce had drifted away as she spent all her free time driving her father to chemo and doctor appointments. She did have a few college friends who would be willing to let her stay, but they lived in other states.

"No family, and I wouldn't want to put my friends in danger." That was true, but it would have been nice to have someone she could turn to. If not for a place to stay, then at least for emotional support.

"It'll have to be a hotel, then. If you want to pack a few things, I can give you a ride to one."

"I can take a taxi," she responded, walking to the spare room and pulling a duffel from the closet. A few of her father's things were still there. The old satchel he'd carried to work for decades. His favorite tie. A couple of shirts with quirky graphics that he'd loved to wear.

"Do you have a roommate?" Detective McGregor asked, his gaze on the tie that hung from a hook.

"My father lived here for a while."

"I thought you had no family?"

"He passed away. Cancer."

"I'm sorry," he said, his dark eyes warm and understanding.

She looked away, focusing on getting the duffel, because she wasn't used to sympathy. Until recently, she hadn't told many people about her mother. She had wanted it to fade like a bad dream. Co-workers knew about her father, but they had tiptoed around the cancer diagnosis and treatment like it was a taboo subject. "Thank you. It was hard to lose him, but I was glad I got a chance to say good-bye," she said as she carried the bag to her room.

"That's the hardest part about losing someone to violence. You don't have a chance to say goodbye or to offer another *I love you*."

Surprised that he would be so open about something so personal, she met his eyes. "That was one of the most difficult things about losing my mother. It felt unfinished. As if the timer had been stopped before the end of the game."

"That's a good way to put it." He smiled, crossing the room and closing the curtains. "King and I will be out in the living room when you're ready to leave."

He walked into the hall, King padding along beside him.

Instead of opening her closet or dresser and grabbing the things she needed, she watched him leave. She had wanted to interview him for her show. Now she just wanted to talk to him. To find out more about how he had grown from his tragedy into a successful, compassionate person.

"Don't even think about it, Sasha," she muttered, tossing a few things into the duffel and telling herself she wasn't at all

interested in getting to know Bradley Mc-
Gregor on a personal level.

Sasha knew how to get ready quickly.
She had a duffel packed and was out of
the bedroom in just under fifteen minutes.
"I'm ready," she said as she walked toward him, gripping her bag in her left
hand. No ring on her finger. He noticed.
Not because he was interested in dating,
but because noticing details was what he
did. Partially because he was trained to do
so. Partially because he had learned how
important details were the year his parents
were murdered. He had been the primary
and only suspect for just long enough to
make him paranoid about keeping track
of his whereabouts, noting the people who
were around him, what they were wearing, doing, how they were acting. What
was said by whom at what time. His mind
was constantly humming, cataloging details of everyday life, keeping lists. Just in
case he ever found himself on the wrong
side of the interview table again.

It was a great tool in the work he did as a detective for the NYPD, but it didn't always serve him well in his daily life. He'd had more than one person tell him he was too serious, that he didn't know how to have fun, that he was too devoted to his job, too focused on making sure the justice system worked the way it was intended to. He got the bad guys off the street. The court system made sure to keep them there.

In a perfect world, that would work perfectly.

But it wasn't a perfect world.

Sometimes, the bad guys slipped through the cracks and did more damage, caused more hurt. Sometimes, innocent people were tried and found guilty. The day he'd joined the police force, he'd promised himself that he would do everything he could to prevent either of those things from happening.

Yes. He took his job seriously, but that was because he understood just how damaging false accusations and arrests could be.

"Are we waiting for something?" Sasha prodded, her smile a little too bright.

She was nervous, her foot tapping impatiently on the floor, her knuckles white from her too-tight grip on the bag.

"That's not much," he said, gesturing to the duffel. "Are you sure you don't want to pack a suitcase?"

"I can come back, if I need to be away for more than a couple days." She strode to the door and held it open. "I'm not trying to rush you, Detective, but I start my day early."

"Your cable show airs in the morning?" he asked.

He knew it did.

He'd watched it a few times since she had visited the precinct and tried to get him to agree to an interview.

"Yes. I usually leave my house by five." She hiked the bag onto her shoulder, her bright-colored coat riding up her slim hip.

"That will work out well."

"In what way?"

"Tomorrow is my day off. I can pick you

up at the hotel." He stepped into the hall, allowing King to move ahead of him, and watched as the Malinois sniffed the air.

"There's no need for you to go to the trouble, Detective."

"You can call me Bradley. That's what my friends call me."

"I appreciate your help tonight, but I can't expect you to keep escorting me from one location to another."

"Do you have a better plan for staying safe?" he asked. King seemed relaxed, his scruff flat, his tail wagging, but he was watching Bradley intently.

"Not now, but I'll think of something before tomorrow morning."

"And if you don't?"

"I'll figure something out. I'm resourceful." She smiled, walking downstairs and to the front door.

"How about this? If you come up with a better plan, call me. If you don't, I'll pick you up at 4:30." He took out a business card. It was time for their evening run, an activity that they both needed after a long day of work. Once he got Sasha safely to a hotel, he'd go home, change and run down to the bay front. At night, this time of year, it was chilly and damp near the water. Not weather most people enjoyed being out in, but Bradley enjoyed the relative quiet of early autumn evenings. Compared to long summer days when warm weather drove Sheepshead Bay residents to the shore, fall was a deterrent that allowed him to have the solitude he sometimes craved.

She nodded, not agreeing to the plan, but taking the card and shoving it in her coat pocket. He thought she was going to open the door and step outside, but she hesitated with her hand on the knob.

"I hope he's not out there," she murmured, pressing her eye to a peephole in the door.

"If he is, I doubt he'll try anything with King and I so close."

"He did when we were at the bakery," she pointed out.

"We were in a building. He was outside.

The windows and walls between us gave him a false sense of bravado."

"Or he is crazy enough not to care about being caught."

"He cares. If he didn't, he wouldn't have run when King and I went after him. Ready to go?"

"Sure. Why not?"

Bradley was relieved. He understood her desire to stay in her apartment. As she'd pointed out, she had a life to live. A job, friends, people who depended on her. Continuing with her routine and going about her daily activities probably felt like the right thing to do, but it would be dangerous to live life as if a stalker wasn't after her. The fact that she was willing to go to a hotel was a step in the right direction, as far as protecting her went.

But she would also be alone.

No friends or family who could offer her a safe place to stay until her stalker was caught.

That had surprised him.

She seemed upbeat, peppy and warm-hearted. The kind of person who probably attracted a lot of attention everywhere she went. Not because of her looks—though she was beautiful—but because of her bright eyes and wide smile. She exuded kindness the way others exuded hate and animosity. He'd worked in law enforcement for so many years, he sometimes forgot people like Sasha existed. Then he would meet someone like her and be reminded that not everyone had an angle or an agenda. Some people were just good-hearted.

Unless she did have an angle.

She had wanted his story.

She had asked for an interview.

It was possible she was still after those things.

The cynic in him was all too aware of that fact.

He reached past her and opened the door, motioning for her to stay where she was as he and King stepped outside. The evening was quiet aside from the soft hum of distant traffic and muted honk of horns.

New York City never slept, but neighborhoods like this one did.

He watched King, noting the Malinois's relaxed body and perked ears. King gave no indication of danger as they made their way to the cruiser. An intelligent and protective dog, he had been trained to do what he was bred for: protect and apprehend. If there was danger, he always let Bradley know. As far as partners went, he was as good as any human partner Bradley had ever had.

He opened the back hatch of the cruiser. King jumped into his crate and settled down for the ride.

"He knows the routine," Sasha commented as Bradley opened the passenger door and waited for her to climb in.

"We've been working together for a couple years. He loves his job, but he also loves the end of the day when he knows we're heading home for our run." He took the duffel from her hands and set it in the back seat.

"He runs after a full day of work?"

"He has to. Otherwise, he'd be getting me to play ball all night." He smiled and closed the door.

The night was still quiet, the soft chirp of crickets mixing with the muted sound of traffic. To Bradley, it was the music of autumn, the brisk air and crunch of dry grass under his feet reminding him of his childhood. He had grown up in the city, and he loved it. The first fourteen years had been rocky. His parents had been drug addicts who cared more about their next fix than they did about their kids. He had been constantly hungry and constantly trying to find ways to keep his sister fed and healthy. Ten years younger than him, Penelope had been four when their parents were murdered. She had been the sole survivor of the crime. He had been the first suspect.

He tried not to let those early years of neglect and hunger and want affect him. He tried not to dwell on the fact that he had been suspected in his parents' murders before he was even old enough to drive. He didn't want that to change his attitude about people. He didn't harbor bitterness or hate. His parents—the ones who had raised him and his sister after the murders—had taught him grace, forgiveness and love. But there was no way to unlive those first few days after his parents died. There was no way he could ever forget the way the people in his community had looked at him—with suspicion and unease. For years after he was cleared of the crime, there had been rumors about him. Those rumors had ramped up again after the copycat murder several months ago. That case had led to the arrest of his parents' killer. Randall Gage was now behind bars. Where he belonged. However, the copycat murderer—someone who had killed a married couple and left their three-year-old daughter as the sole witness—was still at large.

Right now, finding the killer was Bradley's focus and mission. The little girl, Lucy Emery, had been able to give a vague description of the killer—just as his own sister had twenty years earlier: a man wearing a clown mask with blue hair. But a couple of months ago, Lucy had started saying she "missed Andy." Her aunt Willow and her husband, Detective Nate Slater, Bradley's colleague at the Brooklyn K-9 Unit, who'd taken Lucy in, had said there was no one named Andy in Lucy's life. Maybe Andy was someone from the neighborhood who knew Lucy. Maybe he'd seen how neglectful her parents had been. Maybe Andy was the masked killer.

For months, the team had been questioning people in the Emerys' neighborhood, trying to find someone who was familiar with Andy. Bay Ridge was tight-knit and often close-lipped, but the people there wanted the killer caught. Most had been forthright about what they had seen and heard the night of the murder. Thus far, not one person knew of an Andy who had hung around the Emery house or who might have known Lucy and her parents.

Chasing one dead-end lead after another was frustrating, but Bradley wasn't willing to give up. Someone knew something. That was the way it always was with crime. Sooner or later, he would get the answers he was looking for.

He was hoping for sooner.

He didn't want Lucy to grow up in the shadow of the unknown as he and Penny had. He wanted to give her and her aunt the answers they deserved.

With Sasha safe in the passenger seat, he stayed outside the vehicle to make a quick call to his sister, Penny, just to check in. Something he did every day when he hadn't seen her much that day and always would. Even though his kid sister was a grown woman and engaged now to a great guy and someone Bradley trusted with her life, Detective Tyler Walker, he still liked to touch base and make certain she was doing okay.

Growing up in a neglectful and unloving home had made him conscious of the importance of expressing and showing love to the people he cared about. He hadn't wanted Penny to ever feel like he had—that she was an afterthought and expendable.

Tyler had been instrumental in getting their parents' murderer thrown into jail, and Bradley was confident he would spend the rest of his life making certain Penny never felt alone or unloved.

But he still made his phone call.

She didn't answer, and he left a brief message. He slid into the driver's seat, scanning the cars parked along the street as he pulled away from Sasha's apartment. No headlights went on. No car pulled out behind him. The man who had been outside Sasha's house had disappeared into the night, but Bradley knew he would be back. Stalkers didn't give up hunting their prey.

"I appreciate you doing this, Detective Bradley," Sasha said, breaking the silence.

"It's no problem," he responded. "Any thought as to what hotel you want to stay at?"

"I probably should have one, but I've

been preoccupied. I guess whichever one is closest."

"How about one that's close to the K-9 unit?" he suggested. "We may need further information from you. That will make it easy to pick you up and escort you to the offices."

"That's fine."

"Great," he said, turning in that direction.

Traffic was heavy, rush hour well underway.

It would have taken less time to walk the few miles to the hotel he had in mind, but he didn't want to risk it. He had no idea where Sasha's stalker lived or how far he had gone when he'd run from King.

Better to be safe now than to be sorry later.

He'd drive her to the hotel and escort her inside.

Then he would go home and try to put the day's events out of his head. Just for a little while. Clear his head as he pushed his body to run, because he didn't want to be consumed by his job the way his parents had been consumed by their addictions. He wanted to live a life dedicated to more than that. His sister would be getting married soon. She'd be moving out of the house they had shared for years, and he would be living alone for the first time in his life.

He hadn't decided how he felt about that.

He only knew that changes were coming. For better or worse, life would be different. He wanted to embrace it, enjoy it and appreciate it for what it was.

But he also wanted to pursue justice.

He wanted to make certain the community he loved was safe.

That meant putting murderers like Randall Gage in jail—which he'd done last month with the help of the Brooklyn K-9 Unit and unexpected sources, like Randall's cousin Emmett Gage, a US marshal now engaged to his coworker Belle Montera, a K-9 officer. A DNA match on a genealogy site had led the K-9 unit to Emmett, knowing he was a relative of the killer. And hard as it had been for Emmett to accept that someone in his family was a murderer, he'd gotten Randall Gage's DNA so that it could be matched against a sample taken from evidence left at the crime scene. Finally, after twenty years, a very cold case had been solved.

Keeping Brooklyn safe also meant finding out who Andy was.

And protecting innocent people from danger.

Tomorrow was his day off. He planned to spend part of it questioning the Emerys' neighbors again. The rest of it he'd spend making sure Sasha's stalker didn't have another chance to take a shot at her.

FOUR

Sasha's alarm went off at 3:30 a.m.

She was already awake. She had been for hours.

The hotel room was quiet and clean, the bed comfortable, but every time she had shut her eyes, she had seen Martin Roker's face. The hooked nose and light blue eyes, slumped shoulders and rangy body.

She shuddered as she ran a brush through freshly washed and dried hair and pulled it back into a high, tight ponytail. The woman in the mirror was pale, her eyes deeply shadowed. Fine lines fanned out from her eyes, and what looked like a frown line marred the skin between her brows.

She rubbed at the spot, grimacing a little

at the visage in the mirror. She was just a few years younger than her mother had been when she had died. She couldn't remember her having wrinkles and lines. She remembered her smile, her laugh. Sometimes, she remembered her voice.

But wrinkles?

No. Her mother hadn't had those.

"But you sure do," she muttered.

A little mascara and some lip gloss, and she was as ready as she was going to be for work.

She brushed her hand down her cotton blouse. Royal blue with long sleeves. No pattern. She'd donned a black pencil skirt that hugged her curves without drawing attention to them. She wasn't on cable television to bring attention to herself. She wanted to draw the public's attention to the good things that were happening in the community. To bring a little brightness into what could sometimes be a dark and frightening world. The show was low-budget. She didn't get paid much for her work, but Sasha didn't care. For the first time in years, she felt like what she was doing mattered.

She glanced at her watch. Ten of four.

She'd have the hotel concierge call her a taxi. That would save Bradley a trip to the hotel. She wasn't sure if he lived in Sheepshead Bay. It didn't really matter. He'd said this was his day off, and she didn't want him to get up early to escort her to work.

A taxi there. A quick run into the building.

She would be fine.

And she would be avoiding spending more time with a man who had taken up too much of her thoughts during the long sleepless night. Bradley McGregor was not what she had expected. The brief meeting they'd had at the K-9 headquarters a couple of weeks ago had given her the impression that he was gruff, hard-edged and serious.

She still thought he was those things, but she had seen compassion in his eyes. She had heard warmth in his voice. He wasn't as hard as he might want people to think, and that had made her more curious than she should probably be.

She wasn't in the market for a relationship.

She certainly wasn't going to get involved with someone when her life seemed to be spinning out of control.

That being the case, staying away from a guy like Bradley seemed prudent.

She fished in her coat pocket, searching for and finding his business card. She hated to call so early, but she wanted to catch him before he left to pick her up. Before she could dial the number, someone knocked on the door.

She jumped, the card falling from her suddenly numb fingers.

"Who's there?" she called as she hurried to the door.

"Bradley McGregor."

She peered out the peephole.

He was standing a few feet away, hands in the pockets of a wool coat, King standing beside him.

She unlocked the door and opened it, stepping back to let them in. "I was just going to call you," she said, the words coming out too quickly.

She was nervous.

She didn't know why.

She talked to people all the time.

Interviewed men, women and children without giving a thought to the fact that they were strangers.

Right now, though, looking into Bradley's dark brown eyes, she felt tongue-tied and discomfited and gauche, all her well-rehearsed icebreakers gone.

"Were you?" he asked, giving King a command to lie down as he closed the door.

"I didn't want you to waste your time coming out to get me. You did say 4:30. I thought I'd catch you before you left."

"Do you have a ride?" he asked, his gaze dropping from her face to her pencil skirt and stocking-clad feet.

"I was going to call a taxi." She hurried to the duffel, pulled out her heels and slid into them, using that as an excuse to stop looking into his eyes.

"A taxi?"

"One of those vehicles you hire to take you places?" she quipped, turning to face him again.

He was in casual clothes. Faded jeans, a long-sleeved T-shirt, scuffed leather work boots and a wool coat that he'd left open. He looked relaxed, his hands tucked into the pockets of his coat, a smile tugging the corner of his lips. "Thanks for the lesson in city transportation," he said. "But I'm wondering why you were planning to call a taxi when you knew I was coming to pick you up."

"Like I said, I didn't want you to be bothered. Especially not on your day off."

"I don't mind being bothered," he responded. "And I'll feel better knowing that you had someone walk you through the hotel and outside."

"That's nice of you, but I'm used to doing things on my own. I've been living in the city for ten years. I've got things figured out."

"During how many of those years was a stalker after you?" he asked.

"That's been a recent thing."

"So, maybe having an armed escort should also become a recent thing," he replied. "Do you need more time to get ready? King and I can wait in the hall. I only knocked because I saw the light under the door."

"No. I'm good." There was no sense putting off the inevitable and no good reason to send him away. He was already awake. Already out of his house. She might as well accept that and move on. Stalker or not, she had a job to do.

"Anything happen last night?" he asked.

"No. It was quiet. To be honest, I felt safer here than I've felt at home the last few days."

"You've been worried about the Roker look-alike."

It wasn't a question, but she nodded.

"How could I not be? He looks just like a dead man."

"A dead man who murdered your mother."

"Exactly. I have no idea what he wants with me, but I can't believe it's anything good."

"He proved that yesterday."

"Did your team find any useful evidence at the scene?" she asked as they stepped into the hall.

"Nothing that is going to help us identify him. No DNA evidence. No fingerprints." He frowned. "Once your workday is over, I'd like you to stop by the K-9 unit. We'll need your formal statement. I'd also like you to look at a lineup of suspects."

"I thought you said your team wasn't able to get evidence that would lead to identifying the man?"

"They weren't, but we may have some ideas."

"I can stop by after work. That's not a problem," she said. King was a few feet ahead, his tan fur soft-looking, his tail high. He loped rather than walked, his lithe body seeming to hum with pent-up energy. If he noticed anything unusual, he didn't indicate it. That should have made her feel better, but she was still anxious as Bradley pushed the elevator button and she waited for the doors to open.

She wasn't sure what she expected to see.

Maybe Martin Roker standing in the elevator, a gun in hand.

But when the doors slid open, the elevator was empty.

She stepped in, edging back as King and Bradley followed.

"You're still nervous around King," Bradley commented.

"Why would you say that?"

"Because you're staring at him as if you expect him to jump up and take a chunk out of you."

"I don't. It's just…"

"What?" He pushed the lobby button, and the doors slid closed.

"I haven't spent much time around dogs.

We didn't have one when I was a kid, and I haven't had time for one as an adult."

"You work a lot of hours?"

"I do five live programs and tape two shows for the weekend. That takes time. Plus, research and prep work. I do a lot of that at home, but it still takes a lot of my time and attention."

"Your boss won't let you bring a dog to work?" he asked.

"I never asked. She probably wouldn't mind. Prudence is happy as long as my ratings stay up, and I'm getting my job done. I'm just not sure it would be fair to have a puppy in an apartment."

"You mean like most dog owners in New York City?" he asked with a smile that took any condemnation from his words.

He had a nice smile. One that made laugh lines appear at the corners of his eyes and softened the hard edges and sharp angles of his face.

"Yes. I suppose I do," she responded, laughing a little. "I've always wanted a dog. I just don't know much about them, and I have no idea what would be a good fit for my lifestyle."

"Most dogs are very happy to fit into whatever lifestyle they're offered. Take King, for example," he said.

The Malinois turned his eyes, his mouth opening in what looked like a doggy smile.

"He loves to work. He loves to play. He loves anything that requires him to be on the go. He's a perfect working dog, but he also is a great companion at home. Once he wears off some of his energy. I take him for runs to make certain that happens. On our days off, we go to parks and hike. I let him jump in ponds and act like the goofball he is. He thanks me by not tearing apart my furniture and walls."

She laughed again, trying to picture the serious dog acting like a puppy. She wanted to ask how long the two had been working together, how old King was and how Bradley had gotten involved in K-9 work, but the elevator doors opened, and all his warmth and good humor seemed to slip away.

Even in casual clothes instead of a suit, he suddenly looked like a detective, his focus sharp and intent, his gaze scanning the lobby as they walked through it.

She hadn't thought she needed or wanted him there.

She had been convinced that she could make her way to work on her own with only a small twinge of fear and anxiety, but her heart was slamming against her ribs as he led her into the hotel parking garage, her mouth dry with fear.

"I'm glad you came," she said, the words slipping out unintentionally. She was glad, but she didn't want to sound needy. She certainly didn't want him to think that she expected him to play bodyguard to her.

"Scared?" he asked.

"I'd be lying if I said I wasn't."

"Caution isn't a bad thing, Sasha. I don't think the man who has been stalking you knows you're here, but that doesn't mean we shouldn't act as if he does."

"I don't want to live in fear. I did that for a while after my mother died. I was almost too afraid to function. Knowing that she was alive one minute and gone the next changed my sense of safety and security and my view of the world." She shrugged, not wanting to say more. She had never told anyone about the dark months after her mother died. About the way she had jumped at shadows, woken from nightmares and expected the boogeyman to jump out of every closet. Even her father hadn't known. He had expected her to soldier on. Just like he had. "I didn't want you to be bothered on your day off."

"I understand that. I had similar feelings after my parents' murders." He frowned. "That's off the record."

"Bradley, I would never use anything you told me on my show. You've already made it clear you don't want to be interviewed, and I respect that."

"Sorry. I'm a little jaded about the press."

"You weren't treated fairly after your parents were murdered, so I understand."

"How do you know? You were what? Five?"

"Twelve, but I don't remember the news story. I did research before I visited you and your sister at the K-9 unit. I'd heard a lot of murmuring from people who thought the Emery murder case was related to your parents. Twenty years after the fact. A preschooler the only witness. The clown mask, the stuffed monkey. You've got to admit, it was eerily similar."

"Trust me, our team spent a lot of time discussing the similarities."

"Then you'll understand the community's fascination and interest. I wasn't planning to contact you or Penelope, but your name kept popping up, and I got curious."

"You know what they say about curiosity, right?" he asked as he led her to a white Jeep and unlocked the door.

"It killed the cat, but you know what they say about cats, right?"

"They have nine lives." He opened the

passenger door, gesturing for her to climb in. As soon as she did, he leaned in so they were face-to-face, eye to eye. She could see threads of deep red in his auburn hair and tiny lines fanning out from his eyes. "Just remember, Sasha. You're not a cat."

He backed away and closed the door.

She waited while he loaded King into a crate in the back, closed the hatch and did a circuit of the vehicle, leaning down a few times to look underneath.

Sasha was antsy, her fingers tapping her thigh, her body humming with the need to move. She was used to going top speed all day, five days a week. Even her Saturdays were busy. Cleaning, errands, research.

Sundays, she tried to rest, but there were always things to be done before and after church. Coffee with the Bible study group. Doughnuts for the worship team. She often stopped by the hospital where her dad had spent so much time during his last year, bringing treats to the nursing staff.

That didn't leave much time for introspection.

That was how she had always liked it.

Lately, though, as she researched her mother's murder case and readied herself to tell the story most people had never heard, she had wondered if she were still running from fear and sadness. Every time she tried to record her story, she found reasons to not do it. She had told her producer she would air it as a two-part show on a weekend. Prudence had suggested it be presented on the anniversary of her mother's death, and Sasha had foolishly agreed.

That date was looming large.

Just two weekends away, and she had nothing recorded.

So, put it on your calendar, and get it done, she told herself, pulling out her phone and making a note as Bradley climbed into the driver's seat. "Everything okay?" she asked absently, not really expecting an answer.

"Just checking for a bomb," he replied.

Dead serious.

Not a hint of humor in his voice.

She met his eyes. "You're kidding."

"I don't kid about things like that." He started the engine and backed out of the space without further comment.

She was left to her own thoughts.

None of them pleasant.

She had spent days and nights convincing herself she was wrong about being stalked. She could no longer pretend that was true. She could no longer hide her head under the blanket of her busy schedule and hope that the monsters would go away.

She needed to face this head-on, figure out who was after her and why. Only then could she get back to the life she had spent so much time and energy building for herself.

A life she was no longer certain she wanted.

She loved her job. She liked the people she worked with. She enjoyed her neighborhood and city life, but there was a part of her that longed for the family she no longer had and a piece of her heart she wasn't sure could be mended. She wanted to go back to the suburban community she had grown up in and the tiny church where her parents and their parents were buried. Not to stay, but for a visit. She wanted to see it all through the eyes of a mature adult, and she wanted to remember the good times rather than focusing on the dark ones.

Somehow, more than anything, she wanted closure.

The end of the old life that was tied to heartache and tragedy. The beginning of a new one.

She wasn't sure how she would accomplish that, but she thought the very first step was finding out who was stalking her and stopping him.

At this time of the morning, the streets were clear, traffic sparse. A few pedestrians made their way along the sidewalks, staying close to the buildings as they navigated the still-dark world.

Bradley kept his eyes peeled as he pulled up in front of the building that housed Sasha's cable program. Unremarkable but for a small sign near the door, it was in a row of brownstones that had been refurbished and turned into office buildings. Decades ago, the properties on this street had been neglected, windows broken or boarded up, doors listing open from broken jambs. Now it was an upscale area with an eclectic group of shops and a few private residences.

"No need to park or walk me in," Sasha said just as he pulled into a metered space. "The cable programming runs all night. I won't be alone in there."

She seemed to think he planned to drop her off and drive away.

He would have told her that wasn't going to happen, if she'd asked.

"I'll walk you in," he said, getting out of the vehicle and feeding the meter before he opened the hatch and let King out of his crate.

"It's really not necessary, but if you feel the need, that's fine." Sasha hurried past, jogging up cement steps that led to the door.

She used a key to open the door, not that the locked entry made Bradley feel better. Stalkers always found a way.

Even if he didn't know about her stalker, he'd have worried about her coming in before dawn when the area was so desolate—no one around to help her should someone be lurking. "You do this every day?" he asked as he stepped into the building behind her.

"Monday through Friday. Saturday and Sunday are taped during the week. The producer runs them. I usually come in Saturday to prep for the week."

"But it's not required?"

"No. Honestly, my producer would probably be fine if I spent less time here during the week. As long as I'm ready for every broadcast, she's only a stickler for the Monday afternoon meeting."

She strode down the hall, her heels clicking on the tile floor. She'd dressed in a slim-fitting skirt and blouse, her hair pulled back in a ponytail that hung to the middle of her back. Even in heels, she moved quickly.

He walked a few steps to her left, King on the lead beside him. The building seemed empty, the hallway dimly lit, brighter lights flickering on as they moved through. The developer who had refurbished and remodeled the building had done an excellent job, leaving dark wood trim and the ornate 1890 details. The bottom floor had been converted to upscale offices, signs hanging from the closed doors announcing the businesses in stylized letters.

"Nice building," he commented as they jogged up a staircase to the second story. The design here was the same: ornate woodwork and closed doors. On this floor, there were windows that looked into the offices. The lights were off in all but the one near the end of the hall.

"It really is. I'd love to take credit for choosing it for the cable show, but it had nothing to do with me."

"How long have you been working here?"

"A few years. I took the job after I stopped covering the crime beat for a newspaper."

"You worked the crime beat?"

"You sound surprised."

"Just surprised I didn't meet you during that time."

"I was covering Manhattan, so I'm not surprised we didn't run into each other," she responded as they reached the door at the end of the hall. A fire exit was beside it, a poster plastered across it warning that it was alarmed.

"What made you switch jobs?" he asked.

"My father."

"He thought it was too dangerous?"

She gave a quiet laugh and shook her head. "Hardly. My father loved what I was doing. It had been a secret dream of his to be an investigative reporter. He had high hopes that I would one day fulfill that dream for him."

"But?"

"He got sick. Pancreatic cancer. We were on borrowed time, and I didn't want to spend what we had working all hours of the day and night. I quit the job and took a job here. At the time I was just assisting the producer. Normal nine-to-five hours. Not a whole lot of take-home work. She understood my situation, and she gave me ample leave. It worked out well."

"I'm sorry that you lost him to cancer."

"Me, too, but at the end, he was ready to go. Anxious even. He would talk about Mom all the time, about how he was going to see her again soon." She blinked, and he was certain he saw tears in her eyes.

"It still hurts."

"Not as much as it used to, but yes. I'm sure you understand."

"I wasn't close to my folks, but my

adoptive parents were wonderful people. I miss them every day."

"I hadn't realized you were adopted."

"Yes, by the lead investigator on my parents' case. He and his wife took my sister and me in. They were the only people willing to take a chance on a fourteen-year-old boy with a chip on his shoulder. Everyone else who showed interest was willing to take my sister, but not me." He still remembered how it had felt to move in with them, the distrust he had had, the way he had tested their love and their boundaries.

"That's a wonderful story."

"And a true one, but it's—"

"Off the record," she cut in, her hand on the doorknob, her back to him. She was lean and muscular, her body more angular than curved. The kind of woman who would be in a fashion magazine or on a runway rather than a local cable news program.

"I was going to say it's the truncated version. There were a lot of tough times before there were good ones. I gave everyone who met me a run for their money. But you're right. It's all off the record."

"Like I said, I heard you loud and clear when you said you didn't want to do an interview or tell your story. I respect that. We'll have to be quiet when we go in. They're shooting a program, and it's not a large space. Sound carries, if we're not careful." She stepped into the office, holding the door so he and King could follow.

It was as bare-bones as he'd seen in any building. A love seat under the window that looked into the corridor, a chair sitting against one wall. An old wooden coffee table sat in the center of the ten-by-twelve reception area, a few thumbed-through magazines cluttering its surface.

A reception desk blocked access to several file cabinets and a door that led into a hallway. No receptionist. Just a phone sitting dejectedly near a powered-down computer.

"The receptionist doesn't arrive until nine," Sasha said quietly as she shrugged out of her coat and hung it from a hook on the wall beside the desk.

"What are her duties?" he asked, wondering if they actually received calls at a cable show of this size.

"She's basically the producer's assistant. She does whatever is required. Answers phones. Makes appointments. Corresponds with viewers. It's harder than you'd think."

"I didn't think it was easy." He'd be bored out of his mind with a job like that. Not because it was easy, but because he'd be stuck in a tiny office all day long with nothing to look at but the walls and the outdated artwork.

"Just a side note, Detective," she said.

"I thought we'd gotten past the formal titles?"

"*Detective* suits you," she replied with a smile. "We'll go to my office. It's really just a glorified closet, but I'm glad to have it. No talking in the hallway when that red light is on." She pointed to a light above the door that glowed bright red.

"Got it."

"I'm more worried about King."

At the mention of his name, King's ears perked up, and he grinned.

"Don't be. He only barks when there is something to bark about."

She nodded, but didn't seem convinced, her dark eyes focused on King, her lips pursed. "Behave, King," she said.

King's smile widened, his tongue lolling out.

Sasha laughed quietly and opened the door, stepping into the hallway and moving silently across the carpeted floor. She rounded a corner and opened a door, gesturing for Bradley and King to walk in ahead of her.

She shut the door and sighed. "There. Now we don't have to worry as much. You can have a seat, if you'd like. I'll make a pot of coffee."

She flicked on a coffee maker that sat on a corner of her desk.

If it could be called a desk.

It looked like one of the fold-up tables

they used at church when there was a pot-luck. White top. Metal legs. A laptop computer closed on top of it. A stack of papers to the left of the computer. A coffee cup to the right. There were three file cabinets pushed up against the wall, a small package sitting on one of them. Two chairs were pushed under his side of the table. He pulled one out and sat in it, wincing as he pushed back and hit the wall.

"I told you, it's a glorified closet," she said with a grin.

"At least you have a window," he responded, pointing to a window that seemed centered on a wall.

"Half of one," she pointed out, still grinning. "That's a faux wall the producer got permission to put up. She thinks privacy is good for the creative mind."

"What do you think?"

"I do prefer working alone, so this job has been a great fit."

"What about the production crew? They don't get in the way of your creativity?" he asked, giving King the down-stay command.

"Production crew? You're looking at it. My show is basically live feed. We have a studio and a camera. I set everything up. We have one cameraman who sets up the camera and presses Record. Then he walks out and monitors via a television screen in another room."

"I didn't realize that. I watched the show a couple times, and I was convinced you had an entire team producing it."

"That's nice to know. I always wonder if the people who watch can tell I'm the only one doing everything." She picked up the package. "Wonder what this is."

"Did you order something?"

"Not anything that would be delivered to my office." She set it on the desk and sat, opening the laptop and booting it up before lifting the package again.

"A fan, maybe?"

"They send letters. Not packages."

"Maybe it's an early Christmas gift?"

"It's the beginning of November." She pulled tape from the top of the package.

"No return address. I won't be able to thank them."

Something about that made him lean forward.

Most people included return addresses.

People who didn't preferred to remain anonymous for any number of reasons.

The reasons he was currently thinking about weren't ones that made him comfortable.

"Wait—" he said, but she'd already pulled brown paper away from a white cardboard box. If it had been a bomb, it would have exploded from that alone, so at least he could relax on that end.

"Why?" she asked, using scissors to cut through tape that held the box closed.

"With a stalker, you need to have all packages checked out first. Just in case."

"In case…?" She lifted the lid, her eyes widening, her face draining of color.

"What is it?" He stood, the abrupt movement alarming King. The dog growled, his scruff up, his eyes focused on the door.

Sasha pushed the box in his direction,

then stood and walked to the window, staring out into the darkness.

He expected to see something horrible. A dead mouse. A snake. A threatening note. Instead, there was a flame-colored rose. Orange with burnished red edges to the petals. A little wilted. Otherwise, there was nothing startling about it.

"A rose?" he asked, resisting the urge to lift it from the box.

"My mother's favorite. My father used to give her a dozen just like it for every anniversary and birthday."

"Aside from you," he asked, keeping his tone even and his voice calm, "who else knows that?"

"Now? No one."

"You've never told anyone?"

"Who would I tell?" She turned, her eyes swimming with tears she didn't let fall.

"A boyfriend? Husband? Friend? Co-worker?"

"I don't currently have a boyfriend. I've been divorced for years. And, honestly,

I feel pretty confident when I say you're not someone who likes to talk about the details of your parents' murders. You did, after all, tell me that several times."

"I don't. Not unless I have to."

"It's been the same with me. I've made it a habit to not talk about my mother's murder unless I have to. I'll be telling the story on my cable show, but my focus is going to be on the good that came out of the heartbreak. Certainly not on the details of the loss. There's no way I'd bring those things up while out with friends."

"Murder is definitely not a good dinner conversation."

"Not just murder. Losing anyone you love and talking about it makes people uncomfortable."

She was right.

He could count on one hand the number of people who hadn't shifted uncomfortably when he had mentioned that his parents were murdered. Not that he did often. It wasn't a subject he enjoyed going into, and most people wanted to ask questions he had no intention of answering.

Until recently, he couldn't answer.

Who did it?

Why?

Those questions had haunted him for two decades. Now that their murderer had been apprehended, he wanted to feel closer to some sort of resolution. All he felt was empty. Knowing who had killed his parents didn't change the fact that they were dead. It certainly didn't change him back to the young kid he had been before he had been suspected of their murders. He had hoped to feel closure, and he supposed he did, but he also felt as if the justice he had chased after for so long did nothing to fill the empty parts of his life. The parts that had once been filled with his need for answers, for justice. Maybe even for revenge.

"You think someone who knows about your mother sent this rose?" he asked.

"I have no idea, but it's…odd. Don't you think?"

"Looks like there's a note under the rose. Do you have sterile gloves?" he asked, wishing he'd driven his cruiser. He wanted to read the note, but he didn't want to contaminate evidence.

"In the office first-aid kit. Give me a minute. I'll be right back with them."

She stepped out of the room and ran down the hall.

He followed.

No way was he going to let her wander around an unsecured business on her own. The front door was locked, but there was no doorman as there was in many office buildings. They stepped into the reception area, and she rifled through a desk drawer, pulling out a pack of disposable gloves. "Will these work?"

He nodded and they headed back to her office.

King was still on the floor, head on his paws, eyes fixed on the doorway. He didn't look happy to have been left behind. "Sorry about that, pal," Bradley said, offering him a dog treat he pulled from a bag he carried in his pocket.

"I can't believe he didn't follow us," Sasha said as she pulled gloves from the pack and put them on.

"How about you let me handle that?" he said. "If there's a note that needs to be reported to the police, the packaging, box and everything in it are going to be evidence. We want to do everything we can to preserve them."

"All right." She stepped aside, watching as he put on gloves and carefully lifted out the rose.

Beneath it, a white envelope had been taped to the bottom of the box. He opened it, easing out a sheet of lined paper that had been folded several times. His stomach lurched when he realized what he was looking at.

Letters written in dried blood, scrawled across the surface in thick, jagged strokes.

You're next.

FIVE

If Sasha still had a job by the end of the day, she would be surprised. Fifteen minutes after Bradley read the note, the office building was teeming with K-9 police officers and their K-9 partners. Her producer, Prudence Landry, had watched things unfold with a laser-like focus.

Either she wasn't a dog person, or she wasn't a police person, or she simply didn't want to have the morning programming interrupted by a police investigation.

Now she was pacing the hallway, her gaze darting to the recording studio and the green light glowing above its door.

"I hate to try and rush the process, but we have twenty minutes before the next live programming is scheduled to begin," she yelled above the quiet hum of voices that had filled the normally quiet office.

Her husky voice seemed to bounce off the walls, but it had little impact on the officers who were dusting Sasha's office for fingerprints.

"Officers!" Prudence tried again. "Is there a timeline for when you'll be finished here?"

"Sorry about this, Ms....?" a dark-haired cop said as he moved through the hall, a chocolate Labrador retriever at his side.

"Landry. But you can call me Prudence. We're casual around here. Although, not usually casual enough to allow this many dogs at one time." She smiled, but her movements were stiff as she extended a hand.

"They're very well trained," he responded with a charming smile. "I'm Officer Jackson Davison. Emergency services. This is my partner, Smokey."

"It's good to meet you both, but, as I'm sure you'll understand, we have a tight production schedule, and—"

"No worries, ma'am," a female officer said as she packed a few items in a small bag. "We're finished here."

"You are?"

"Aside from the work Smokey and I have to do," Officer Davison said, his gaze skirting past Prudence and landing on Sasha. "You're Sasha?" he asked.

"That's right."

"Mind if Smokey and I take a look at the gift you received?"

"I wouldn't exactly call it a gift," she muttered.

"It's in here," Bradley said, his hand settling on her shoulder, his fingers warm through the soft cotton material.

Her cheeks heated, her stomach doing a crazy little flip.

She wasn't happy with either response, and she stepped away, making room for Smokey and Officer Davison to walk into her office.

The hum of people had faded, officers and their K-9s leaving as quickly as they had come. She assumed they were outside, discussing what they had found. Or maybe they would go back to the K-9 unit first.

"We may as well see what they're doing," Prudence said, hooking an arm through hers and dragging her into the tiny room.

She didn't seem angry.

If anything, she seemed excited and pleased.

"If you don't mind staying there," Officer Davison said without looking their way. Smokey was still on the leash, but was sniffing the floorboards near the desk, working his way to the chair and up the leg of it.

Sasha had no idea what he was sniffing for.

She wanted to ask Bradley, but he was near the desk, his gaze focused on Smokey, King lying at his feet.

Smokey's tail wagged twice. Then his head popped up, his nose moving closer to the edge of the desk. He put his front paws on the chair, extending his head over the desk, before he retreated, trotted around the desk and repeated the process.

Once.

Again.

Around the desk. Up. Sniff. Drop down.

Finally, he seemed to home in on the box that had been placed smack-dab in the middle of the desk. He clawed at the table, trying to get closer.

"Work it out," Officer Davison said.

Smokey hopped onto the chair, front paws on the table, nose centimeters from the box. He sniffed, his tail wagging furiously, then dropped to the ground, lying on the floor and staring at Davison.

"Good boy!" Officer Davison said, pulling a ball from his pocket and leading the dog from the room.

"Good dog, for what?" Prudence asked, her gaze on the box.

"Smokey is a cadaver dog," Bradley explained.

"I hope you're not going to tell me he smells a body in that box," Sasha said, her voice shaking at the thought.

"No, but he just indicated on the box. That means there is more than an excellent chance human blood was used to write the note."

"Human blood?!" Prudence's husky voice was high with surprise.

"That doesn't mean someone died. It just means a small amount of blood was used. The great news is, we can run a DNA test, see if we have a match in the system."

"And if you don't?" Sasha asked, stomach heaving as she watched Bradley place the box in a plastic evidence bag.

"Then we'll find him another way."

"How?" she asked, arms across her chest.

He stared at her.

She stared at the evidence bag.

She'd never been squeamish about blood, but she felt a little sick and very scared.

She had seen the note.

She knew what it said.

You're next.

And she knew who it was from.

Martin Roker's look-alike.

"I need to figure out who he is," she muttered, stepping to the side as Bradley walked into the hall.

He turned quickly, the evidence bag in hand. "You need to do your job, and you need to let me and my team do ours."

"What's that supposed to mean?"

"You're an intelligent woman, Sasha. I'm sure I don't have to explain it to you."

"I'm an intelligent woman who is perfectly capable of making up her own mind about what she should be doing."

"I hate to break in on this little love quarrel," Prudence said wryly, "but your boyfriend is correct. You have a job to do here. Your show airs in two hours, and I haven't seen the script for it."

"First, he's not my boyfriend. Second, my story is prepped and ready. Just like always."

"I'll be back in a few hours, Sasha," Bradley said, ignoring her boss. "If you need anything, though, anything at all, you call me or text me. Okay?"

She could still feel the tension between them, but at least he still had her safety front and center. "I will. Thank you."

She watched him walk away, then turned her attention back to Prudence, her boss's patience clearly low.

"And the story about your mother?" Prudence asked. "I have that scheduled for next Saturday and Sunday. I haven't seen the rough-cut video yet."

"I'm working on it." She was. She just hadn't made much progress.

"Can you have it to me by the end of today?" Prudence asked. "Tomorrow at the very latest."

"Tomorrow is Saturday," Sasha reminded her.

"Yes. Which leaves less than a week for any changes and edits you and I might want. Not to mention that the story of your mother's murder is a hot topic in the news right now."

"It is?" Sasha had avoided watching the news last night and this morning for good reason.

"It started airing on local late-night networks, and it's still running hot this morning. Apparently there was a shooting in Sheepshead Bay last night, and you were involved in it."

"I'm afraid so."

"Don't be. It's great publicity. I have a feeling the ratings for your show are going to skyrocket. Make sure you mention that you'll be telling your story on our cable station next weekend when you broadcast today. I'll leave you to get ready. And I'll make sure the recording studio is empty this afternoon. That way you'll have plenty of time to finish the project." She turned on her heels and marched from the room, obviously more pleased with the chaos in the studio than Sasha would have imagined.

She shook her head, watching as Prudence rounded a corner and disappeared from view.

The office building fell back into its normal quiet. Nothing but the soft hum of the heater to break the silence. She knew she wasn't alone. Prudence was in her office. Darius Warren was in his, putting together notes for his programming the following week. A professor of economics, he broadcast an early-morning State of the Dollar address, highlighting economic trends and giving advice on long-term savings and retirement. After his program, the station ran two hours of paid commercial programming. Mostly advertisements for miracle vitamins or exercise equipment designed for an older crowd. Sasha's program followed that. She usually spent the two hours prior reading over her notes and making sure video clips were ready for her segment. Today's story was on a local teenager who worked odd jobs to earn money to donate to the local animal shelter. Feel-good story about a hardworking teen and cute animals. It should make her audience happy.

She sat at her desk, pulling out her file folder and thumbing through the notes. She needed to focus, but she kept jumping at every sound, her gaze darting to the door, her breath held as she waited for a monster to open it.

"He's not going to enter the building while the police are congregated outside," she reminded herself as she reread a sentence for the tenth time.

Unless he was in the building before you arrived, her brain whispered. Maybe he'd found a way to break in. Or had gotten ahold of a key somehow. Anything was possible.

Her mother had been in a school parking lot when she had been shot. Three of her colleagues had witnessed the murder. Roker hadn't cared. He had been on a mission, and he would have died to achieve it.

He *had* died.

Was Sasha's stalker as driven?

She didn't dare dwell on that. She didn't want an answer to the question. She had a job to do, an audience that was waiting for the next good-news story from New York City. She might not feel cheerful, but no one had to know that. She might be scared out of her mind, but she wasn't going to let that stop her from doing what she had set out to do when she had pitched this idea to Prudence.

"Do your job, Sasha," she muttered. "Then you can worry about everything else."

She pushed every thought from her head that didn't have to do with cute dogs and sweet kittens and guinea pigs squealing in their homes, focusing her energy on something she could control rather than all the things she could not.

Two hours later, she was ready, sitting on the only prop she used—a comfortable velvet-covered armchair that had once belonged to her father. He had never had a chance to see her program, but he would have approved. Each time she sat in the chair, she was reminded of his kindness, his faith, his strength in the face of all that life had brought.

He had never remarried. As far as she knew, he had never even dated after her mother's death. He had poured himself into making certain Sasha felt loved, valued and secure. If she could spread a little of his kindness and optimism, it was the best way to preserve his legacy.

"Ten seconds," the cameraman said, his gruff voice cutting into her thoughts.

She nodded, sliding the folder of notes off-screen, straightening her skirt and blouse, and smiling straight at the camera.

The cameraman held up three fingers. Two. One.

The program began, and she lost herself in the story and her telling of it.

By the time the K-9 team cleared out of the cable news office, King was impatient, whining softly as he sat on the sidewalk beside Bradley. This was their day off. They usually spent it hiking trails at local parks or exploring waterfront areas. King needed the time to run off his energy with a long game of Frisbee or a few laps around a dog park.

"Sorry, boy. I know this isn't what we typically do when we're not on duty, but today is a different kind of day. We have another kind of job." For the past few hours, he'd walked around the building with King, gone around the block in every direction a couple of times, gone into the coffee shops and corner markets that opened up early. No sign of the stalker.

Now he gave King the command to heel and walked up the steps of the brownstone that housed Sasha's office. The sun was rising, the sky tinted gold as the new day stretched across it. Cars whizzed past. Horns honked. Sheepshead Bay was waking, the residents heading to work or returning home after night shifts.

Until yesterday, Bradley had planned to sleep an extra hour, do some laundry and then take King to the dog park. He'd figured they could spend an hour there and then walk to the beach to watch the gulls swoop across the brackish water. That was one of King's favorite pastimes, and Bradley enjoyed watching the Malinois bound across the sand. After that, he had thought he'd wander around the Emerys' neighborhood, listening to gossip and hoping for a lead, particularly on the "Andy" that little Lucy Emery had mentioned, that would bring the K-9 team a step closer to finding the person who had murdered the couple.

Now his focus was on getting Sasha through her workday and back to the hotel without her stalker following them.

He glanced over his shoulder as he rang the buzzer on the intercom panel for the cable channel. His white Jeep was where he'd parked it. Once he made sure Sasha was safely tucked away in the hotel, he planned to go to the K-9 unit to review video footage from several security cameras near the bakery. Yesterday's shooting had been caught on tape. He was certain of that. What he was hoping was that there was a clear view of the perp's face.

The street behind him was filled with commuter vehicles and taxis, all vying for a position in the burgeoning rush-hour traffic. Dim morning light filtered through a thin cloud cover. It would be a rainy, windy day in the city.

If only bad weather kept criminals at home.

"WBKN," a woman's voice said through the intercom. "May I help you?"

He identified himself and was buzzed in, not liking that anyone could get inside by saying he was a cop. Inside, Bradley jogged up to the second floor. Sasha wasn't in her office. She broadcast live at eight every morning. He glanced at his watch, then walked the hall until he located the broadcasting studio. A large window opened into a spare room. White walls and a backdrop that hung from the ceiling near the far wall. No exterior windows. A camera set on a tripod pointed at a lone chair, a man behind it hunched over and focused in Sasha's direction. She sat in the chair, leaning forward and staring into the camera's lens as if she were looking into the eyes of her best friend.

Bradley couldn't hear what she was saying, but he watched her hands move as she smiled into the camera. She was animated and filled with enthusiasm for her subject. The kind of television personality people would feel connected with and want to continue watching.

Had her show put her in the crosshairs of a madman?

She was being stalked and taunted by someone.

Bradley had consulted with the team. None of them believed the gunman had been trying to kill her. She had been close enough for a clean shot. Even through the storefront window. So, what had been the point? To terrify her? To bring the stalker to the forefront of her mind?

Obsession was the hallmark of a stalker's personality, and the person who had sent the rose was obsessed enough to have found out information that Sasha was certain only she knew.

Obviously, she was wrong.

Someone knew about her mother's love of that color rose. The package was proof positive. The note had been sent to the forensic lab and would be swabbed for DNA. Maybe that would bring them some answers. In the meantime, Bradley would question Sasha again. Maybe she would remember something important. A person she had spoken to. A place where her mother had been mentioned. Perhaps she'd talked about it during one of her broadcasts without realizing it.

He frowned.

He could believe a lot of things, but not that. When he spoke of his parents' murders or even just his parents, he remembered. It was something he didn't do often enough for it to become commonplace. It certainly wasn't something he would do without giving it serious thought.

He had a feeling Sasha was the same. She had said very little about her mother's murder, providing just enough information to explain who she thought she had seen.

Martin Roker.

A dead man.

Impossible, and yet she had been lucid in her description of the man who she had said looked exactly like her mother's killer.

Unaged.

Unchanged.

Well, if the blood on the note did link to DNA, they'd soon know if Roker had an identical twin no one had known about. Or maybe a similar-looking son. There wasn't much information on the guy other than him having an estranged wife and daughter.

She finished speaking and settled back in the chair, her ponytail hanging over her left shoulder, her hands idle in her lap. Her smile slipped away as a monitor high on the wall to her left flickered to life, showing a quick glimpse of Sasha before switching over to a news clip featuring a local humane society and a teenage boy who was wheeling a wagon filled with bags of dog and cat food through the door.

Sasha's focus was on the screen, her body tense as she watched the clip. As it ended, she brushed her ponytail back off her shoulder, focused on the camera and smiled.

The cameraman lifted his arm, showing three fingers.

Two.

One.

Sasha began speaking again, her smile bright and animated. She looked nothing like the tense woman who had watched the video clip. Whatever she was feeling, whatever she'd been thinking, was well hidden behind her peppiness.

He watched until the end, waiting as she settled back into the chair, her eyes on the flickering monitor on the wall. A few credits appeared, there and gone so quickly he wasn't sure anyone would have time to read them.

After a moment, the screen went black and she stood, stretching a kink out of her neck, her body lithe and slender, her hair sliding along her shoulders. She rubbed her neck and stifled a yawn, lifting a folder from the floor to her left and saying something to the cameraman. Bradley thought he heard a deep chuckle and a higher, more feminine one.

As if she sensed his focus, Sasha's attention shifted to the window, her eyes widening.

She waved and smiled.

The cameraman turned toward the window, then stalked to the door and opened it.

"Who are you?" he demanded as Sasha edged out behind him.

"He's...a friend of mine."

The cameraman scowled, his ruddy face nearly covered by a full mustache and beard. "I don't like strangers wandering the halls. Even if they are strangers other people know. After that shooting last night, everyone in Sheepshead Bay is on edge. Including me."

"You heard about that?" Sasha asked.

"Who hasn't? I'd have mentioned it sooner, but I figured if you wanted to talk about it, you'd say something."

"I appreciate you giving me time and space to process things," Sasha said, not giving any further details or answering the questions Bradley sensed the cameraman wanted to ask.

People were curious by nature.

When bad things happened, they wanted the details. Not just so they could ogle and gossip, but because they wanted to understand the causes and avoid them.

Sometimes, though, horrible things couldn't be avoided.

Even the best-lived life was sometimes filled with heartache.

Bradley had seen it time and time again. He'd spent one too many late nights or early mornings listening to the heartbreaking sobs of a mother who had lost a child, a father whose daughter wouldn't be coming home, a husband whose life partner would never again kiss him good morning. So many innocent victims of horrible crimes. There were nights when he couldn't sleep, thinking about the heartbreak and sorrow. Only knowing that he could offer help and closure to victims kept him going. The knowledge that there was something better beyond this life was comforting when he stood with grieving loved ones and watched their children, spouses, sisters, brothers or parents being buried.

It was also the impetus that kept him going when he was in the middle of the toughest cases.

Like the murders of the Emerys.

The couple had been killed in front of their three-year-old daughter seven months ago. The sole witness to the crime, Lucy Emery hadn't been old enough to give the kind of details needed for identification or apprehension of the killer beyond the clown mask. The K-9 unit had spent months pursuing one dead-end lead after another.

At first, the residents of Sheepshead Bay had been so busy whispering that the Mc-Gregors' killer was back at it, murdering couples with young children and hoping to get away with it like he had for twenty years, that they hadn't been focused on anything else. Such as the fact that there was a copycat killer at work. But there was such little evidence and nothing to go on. The K-9 unit had been relying on the community to provide insight and information about the Emerys. Whom they associated with, what they did and how they lived their lives were all important factors when it came to tracking down their killer.

Right now, a man named Andy, someone who Lucy had said she missed, was the prime suspect. Clearly, the man had been kind to her in some capacity. But after investigating all possibilities for a couple of months now, the K-9 unit still had no idea who this Andy was or his connection to Lucy or the Emerys. At three, Lucy was just too young to further explain, and talking about him seemed to upset her into silence.

Lucy had been through enough. That was why Bradley had been hoping the people of Lucy's old neighborhood would come through.

Unfortunately, the community hadn't been up-front with information. Every week, Bradley visited the neighborhood and spoke to the people he saw there. Every week, he prayed that there would be a new piece of the puzzle revealed and that, eventually, he'd have the full picture of what had happened the night the Emerys were killed.

So far, it hadn't happened.

Bradley wasn't giving up hope.

After twenty years, his parents' murders had been solved. If that could happen, anything could.

"Right," the cameraman finally said, his bright blue eyes focused on Sasha. "Do you need me to stick around and give you a lift home? After what happened last night, I figure you might not want to walk."

"I appreciate the offer, but I'll be fine," she responded kindly, smiling to take any sting out of the rebuttal.

"You weren't fine yesterday," the cameraman pointed out.

"Yesterday, she didn't have a police officer escorting her," Bradley cut in.

The cameraman shifted his gaze, his expression unreadable as he met Bradley's eyes. "You're with the police?"

"Detective Bradley McGregor. Brooklyn K-9 Unit."

"Good to meet you, Detective. Glad you're going to escort Sasha home. I'm always telling her the streets of Sheepshead Bay aren't as safe as they once were. A beautiful woman like her can't be too careful. Don't you agree?"

"Sure," Bradley responded.

Sasha's cheeks were pink with embarrassment, her fingers curled so tightly around the folder, it was wrinkling beneath her grip.

"Good. Good. Glad we agree. I've got to get ready for the next broadcast. See you tomorrow, Sasha." He threw the last sentence over his shoulder as he walked away.

Sasha didn't respond.

She was already walking back to her office, feet padding lightly on the carpeted floor, skin a shade too pale, shoulders tense.

"Are you okay?" he asked as they stepped into her office.

"Just a little tired. I didn't sleep well last night."

"Ready to head back to the hotel? Maybe you can get some rest?"

"I thought I had to stop at headquarters to give my statement?"

"If you're tired, it can wait."

"Not that tired. More worried than anything. Seeing that rose shook me."

"I'm sure that was what it was intended to do."

"Why?" she asked, dropping into her chair and setting the folder on the table beside her computer.

"Why am I sure?"

"Why would someone want to shake me up?"

"To get your attention. To make sure you know he's there."

"Trust me, I know," she said wryly, her hand shaking as she poured coffee into a white mug near the carafe. "Would you like a cup? I meant to offer it earlier, but things happened."

"I'm good," he responded, watching as she emptied three creamers into the mug, poured several packets of sugar in and stirred it listlessly.

She did look tired, the circles under her eyes dark against her pale skin.

"I don't understand any of this," she said, taking a quick sip of coffee and setting the mug down on the table. "It's been nearly nineteen years since my mother's murder. By this time, I'd think I would be the only person who remembered it."

"It made the headlines when it happened," he reminded her.

"Yes. The scandal made it big news. A woman killed by her ex-love." She shook her head. "My mother made some mistakes. She may have made a lot of them, but she was a good mother, and she did love my father."

"You don't have to explain your family dynamics, Sasha," he said, hating to see the sadness in her eyes. He understood it all too well. He knew the hollowness of loss, the empty place where parents should be but weren't. He'd been fortunate to have adoptive parents who filled that spot better than his biological parents ever had, but just listening to Sasha talk about her mother helped him understand the relationship they'd had. Unlike his parents, Sasha's had loved and cared for her. The affair that had led to murder didn't change that.

"I know. I just think about it sometimes. Especially now that I'm trying to tell my story. I want people to know there is hope after heartache, but the truth is, I'm still broken from the loss of my mother. Death is hard enough, but murder under circumstances like my mother's makes it difficult to mourn properly."

"I understand that."

"Do you?" She sighed, sliding the folder into one of the file cabinets and pulling out another thicker one. "Here is all the information I've collected about my mother's case."

"That's a thick folder."

"The police investigated thoroughly, and they were happy to give me copies of what they had."

She pulled out a crime scene photo, wincing a little as she handed it to him. The second photo she held out was one of a beautiful blonde woman holding a little girl. Both of them were smiling into the camera, their dark eyes dancing with humor. "That's me and Mom. I was five. She was twenty-nine. She was only thirty-eight when she died."

She pulled out a third photo and crowed triumphantly. "Here it is! The picture of Martin Roker."

She slid it across the table, tapping her finger on the face of a gaunt man who was smiling half-heartedly, his attention focused somewhere to the right of the photographer. Blond hair. Hooked nose. Stooped shoulders.

"The man who's been stalking me, who shot at me, looks exactly like him."

"We know he didn't have an identical

twin or any siblings. Maybe he has a look-alike son."

She frowned. "He only has a daughter."

"I'll have our tech guru do some digging into Roker's past. Something's not adding up here."

She nodded. "I wish I knew what he wants with me."

Bradley thought the note had made it clear.

Sasha was next on the kill list of a madman.

He didn't say that. Just pulled out his phone and took a picture of the photo of Roker. "I'm going to send this to both Eden Chang, the tech guru, and my sister, Penny. She's the front desk clerk, but she helps out in record keeping, too, and will get this in your file."

"I spoke with her last week," Sasha said, reminding him of her unscheduled visit and the attempt she had made to get him to agree to an interview.

He hadn't thought much of her then.

As a matter of fact, he had been more

angry than he'd let on. His parents had been gone for twenty years, the killer finally caught, but their murders still seemed to cast dark shadows across his life. No matter how hard he tried, he couldn't seem to get out from under them. "Right. Eden can run this through some face recognition software. Maybe we'll get a match for a current criminal in our data banks."

"That would be strange, don't you think?" She stood, tucking the folder under her arm as she grabbed her coffee.

"What?"

"Roker having a doppelgänger that is a criminal just like him."

"Strange, but not an impossibility. Do you want to go to headquarters now?"

"I hate to keep you here longer, but Prudence is going to have my head on a platter if I don't give her a rough copy of next weekend's story."

"You're going back to the studio?"

"Not the live studio. We have a recording studio. I'll work there. Once I'm finished, I'll set it aside. Tomorrow, I'll cut and edit. If you'd like to wait here, that's fine."

He had the impression that was exactly what she'd like him to do. He might have considered it, but the building was large, the hiding places limitless. There were doors everywhere. Bathrooms on each level. Probably other cubbyholes he hadn't seen.

He had a feeling Sasha's stalker was familiar with the space, that he had been there before, moving down the halls as if he belonged, testing doors, searching for the perfect spot to hide and to spy. Which meant he'd definitely found an easy way in: he had a key.

If he was there now, hiding behind one of the closed doors, King didn't sense it. He walked beside Bradley, his body relaxed, his tail wagging slowly. No stress. No hint that there was anything amiss. Bradley trusted his partner's senses more than he trusted his own, but that didn't mean he was going to let his guard down.

Sasha had every right to feel safe. She had every right to move through her life without threat of harm.

For as long as Bradley could remember, he had rooted for the underdog and fought for the rights of those who couldn't fight for themselves. He thought it came from his early years, when his little sister was a baby, and he was ten, listening to her cry from hunger in the middle of the night while his parents were out partying. He had learned to make bottles. He'd learned how to change diapers. He had learned, by trial and error, to do all the things a good parent should.

He had learned to care for a helpless infant, and from that, he had learned everything else. Compassion. Empathy. Love.

He had built on them during his years with Joe and Allison Brady. Strong Christians who had lived their faith, his adoptive parents had taught him invaluable lessons about forgiveness and loyalty. He carried those things with him every day, using them to be the best law enforcement officer he could be.

Sasha stepped into a room, flicking on a light to reveal stark white walls and the same backdrop he'd seen in the live studio. A camera stood on a tripod against a wall, and she moved it toward the center of the room, focusing it on a comfortable-looking easy chair that sat in the middle of a blue-and-white area rug.

"You can sit in one of those chairs," she said, pointing to two folding chairs that leaned against the wall. He grabbed one and opened it, sitting on the metal seat and giving King the down-stay command.

The Malinois did so reluctantly, offering a quick yawn and soft whine in protest. He wanted to be out chasing gulls. They'd do it eventually. For now, Bradley's focus would stay where it should be: on keeping Sasha safe.

SIX

She spent an hour taping her story, the words pouring out in a rush she hadn't expected and didn't want. So much for the modulated, cheerful voice she had cultivated. Her voice cracked as she explained the way her mother's murder had ripped away her sense of security and destroyed her faith in human nature. It had taken years to overcome that.

And then it had been destroyed again by her ex-husband's infidelity.

She didn't mention that.

It wasn't part of her mother's story. It certainly wasn't something she wanted the world to know.

She didn't want Bradley to know it, either.

He was sitting in a chair, his legs

stretched out and crossed at the ankle, his arms crossed over his stomach. His gaze hadn't wavered since she'd begun speaking, and she found herself, more than once, talking to him instead of the camera.

That wouldn't make for good programming.

Like her modulated voice, she had worked hard at making just the right amount of eye contact with the camera. Not too long or too short. Relaxed mouth and jaw. Easy smile. All the things that made a person seem approachable.

That had been what she had wanted— for people to feel welcomed by the show, drawn into it. She had wanted them to feel encouraged and motivated. She had her show be a call to action and a forum from which people could gain ideas about how they could make a difference in their community.

Prudence often said she had been successful in meeting her goals.

As a matter of fact, there'd been talk of

another slot during the day. Prudence had been toying with the idea of giving Sasha a chance to explore local happenings and do feature stories on book festivals, grand openings, school theater productions.

Sasha had liked the idea, but she hadn't been as excited by the potential opportunity as she had thought she should be.

That was what she'd wanted, right? To build a career in the news industry, working as a journalist who saw the world through a different lens and reported on it?

She had thought so.

Until she had begun digging into her own story.

The more she had uncovered about her mother's murder, the more she had learned about her past, the less certain Sasha had been about her future. Looking through her mother's things, reading through old journal entries, seeing the soft looping handwriting and the flowery phrases, had reminded her of the things she'd once jotted in her own journal, the dreams she had once had.

She had wanted to be a photojournalist, traveling the world to take pictures of exotic locations and animals and people. She had wanted to use a camera to capture the world and give it as a gift to other people.

Instead, she sat in a small room, making a video recording of her mother's story.

Her father's.

Hers.

They were interconnected, held together by their family relationship and by tragedy.

She was the last person alive who had seen her parents during their happy years. After the affair, before the murder, they'd been working hard to rebuild their marriage.

Sasha had been old enough to notice the way they had looked into each other's eyes, the secret that passed silently between them. The smiles. The passionate kisses they hadn't realized she'd seen. Their love for each other had made her feel secure and safe. The ending to the story was a tragic one, but there had been a lot of beauty in the middle of that.

She planned to convey that in the recording, but her voice wobbled as she attempted to describe the love between her parents, her eyes burning with tears.

She wasn't a pretty crier.

She was the kind with the red nose and the blotchy skin.

Definitely not something the world needed to see, but she couldn't seem to pull it together. The more she tried not to cry, the more she wanted to do it. She could almost picture her mother as she'd been the last day. They'd both been heading out the door. Sasha had been in her sophomore year of high school. Her mother had been a creative writing teacher at the local middle school. They'd said goodbye as they'd walked out the door. Exchanged hugs and "I love you"s like they did every day.

Everything had been normal and good.

And then it hadn't been.

She cleared her throat, forcing herself to

keep talking, spewing out the script she had written and memorized. She felt like she was choking on the words, her throat clogged with the disappointment and grief she hadn't allowed herself to feel in years.

She stood up, blindly walking to the camera and turning it off. She'd had enough for today. Maybe for every day.

"You okay?" Bradley asked quietly. He had moved from the chair to her side and was studying her face as if there were secrets he could read there.

"I'm fine. Just tired." Her voice was still husky, the words sandpaper-rough.

"Do you always cry when you're tired?" he asked, brushing a tear from her cheek.

"Only when I'm talking about my mother." She swiped tears from her face, impatient with her weakness and embarrassed that Bradley had seen it.

"You're braver than I am," he commented, cupping her shoulder and urging her into the hall.

"How so?"

"You asked if I'd do an interview for your show. I refused."

"Because you're a private person who doesn't enjoy his past being dragged into the present," she said.

"That's only part of the reason."

"What's the other part?"

"Talking about it is too painful. Not just because my parents were murdered, but because their deaths barely left a hole in my life. The truth is, there were days after they died when I was thankful they were gone, because I was certain my sister would have a better life with just about anyone else than she'd had with them."

"What about you?" she asked.

"Me?"

"Did you think you'd have a better life?"

He studied her solemnly, his dark eyes shadowed with memories of the past. "At the time, Penny was my sole focus. I'd been taking care of her the best way I could from the time she was an infant, but I was smart enough to know it wasn't enough. She didn't just need a big brother who made sure she ate and bathed and had clean clothes to wear. She needed a stable environment, a home where there weren't empty beer cans lying on the floor and used needles in the bathroom trash can."

"I'm sorry, Bradley. That's no way for a child to grow up."

"No, it isn't. I wanted better for her, but I had no idea how to provide it."

"I wasn't talking about your sister. I was talking about you," she corrected.

His jaw tightened, his lips pressing together.

She thought he was going to speak. Instead, he opened the door and urged her into the hall. "Do you need to go back to your office?" he asked.

"No. I've got everything I need to work on here." She held up the folder. "And I packed my home laptop. I can work from the hotel room."

"Do you need anything at your house?"

She could think of several things she would have liked to get. A couple of books. Her e-reader. The photo of her parents that she kept on her bedside table.

"No," she said, deciding against mentioning any of those things. Bradley had spent his entire morning babysitting her. They still had to stop at the K-9 unit before he dropped her at the hotel. The last thing she wanted to do was give him more to do on his day off.

"You're sure? I don't mind stopping there."

"I'm sure."

"If you change your mind, let me know. It shouldn't take long to take your statement. Then I'll drop you off at the hotel."

"I appreciate all you're doing for me. If I can ever repay you—"

"You can," he cut in, his voice a little sharper than it had been.

"Okay. Name it."

"Everything I said to you back there? It stays off the record. Don't use it for any human-interest story or feel-good pieces, okay?"

The fact that he had to say that to her,

that he felt the need to remind her of something he had already said twice, told Sasha everything she needed to know about his opinion of her.

She stopped as they reached the exit, looking straight into his eyes as she spoke. "Just so we're clear, Detective, I didn't hire a man to stalk me, shoot at me and leave notes written in blood on my desk so that I could draw you into my web and trap you there."

His eyes narrowed, the muscle in his jaw twitching. "What's that supposed to mean?"

"Exactly what it sounded like. This isn't some elaborate ruse to get close to you so that I can do a story about the family's tragedy and you and your sister's triumph over it."

"I don't recall saying that it was."

"The fact that you have reminded me three times that our conversations are not on the record said it for you." She pushed open the door and stepped outside, blinking as watery sunlight filled her eyes.

She had forgotten that the sun was up, the street bustling with activity. That time had moved forward while she broadcast her story and recorded a session for next weekend's show.

She strode forward, dodging several pedestrians, and hurried to the Jeep. She wasn't thinking about Roker's double, gunfire or roses the color of fire. She was thinking about getting to the police station, giving her statement and getting away from Bradley as quickly as possible.

She heard the familiar beep as the doors were remotely unlocked. She would have yanked the door open, but a warm, furry body was suddenly pressing against her legs, nudging her away from the door.

"King?" she said, looking down at the tan dog. He was staring into her eyes and growling low in his throat.

She stepped back, tripping on the curb and falling into Bradley's firm chest.

His arm wrapped around her waist, holding her steady as she caught her balance.

"Sorry," she murmured, reaching for the door again.

King butted against her legs, growling and then barking, the ferocious sound scaring her into retreat.

She stepped away from the Jeep. "I don't think he wants me to ride with you," she said, not meeting Bradley's eyes.

She was embarrassed by her outburst and by the anger she'd felt when she had realized how little he thought of her.

She had no reason to feel that way.

They barely knew each other.

She certainly didn't expect him to understand the ethics and morals she lived by, and she knew there were plenty of journalists who would do whatever it took to get a story that would sell.

"I don't think that's the problem," he responded. "What's wrong, King?" he asked.

King barked again, his scruff raised, his tail rigid.

She had seen the dog relaxed and happy.

She had seen him ready to work.

She wasn't sure what she was seeing now. She only knew King wasn't happy.

She stepped onto the sidewalk, watching warily as the dog paced back and forth in front of the Jeep. His nose was to the ground. He'd stopped growling and barking and seemed focused, his head down, his ears back.

"What's he doing?" she whispered, as if talking too loudly might interrupt the dog's concentration.

"I'm not sure," he replied. He was watching King, tracking the dog's movements as he rounded the car and returned. "Something is bothering him. That's all I know."

"Is he sick?"

"No. He's concerned."

"How can you tell?" she asked, her embarrassment fading as he watched the dog work his way from one end of the Jeep to the next. Up onto the sidewalk. A few steps toward the building. Back again.

"The way he is pacing and sniffing. He's trying to work out a problem, but he's not sure what." He dropped to his knees and studied the chassis. "I think I see something."

"What?"

"I'm not sure, and I'm not going to reach in to figure it out. I'm going to call in my sergeant and ask him to come out with one of the detectives who also has bomb detection K-9."

"Bomb detection?" she repeated, because the words didn't make any sense.

There was no way there was a bomb underneath the Jeep.

Was there?

She backed away a few more steps, nearly bumping into a pedestrian.

"Careful," Bradley warned, taking her arm and tugging her back to his side as he pulled out his cell phone.

She tried to hear what he was saying, but traffic was heavy, engines roaring, horns honking, someone yelling. She couldn't hear above the sounds of city life and her own galloping heartbeat.

* * *

Bradley escorted Sasha back inside before the bomb squad arrived. He didn't want her standing out on the sidewalk. If she did, she might as well have a neon sign plastered to her back that read Sitting Duck. A gunman with good aim and the right weapon could take someone out from hundreds of meters away. Sasha could be standing in the middle of a battalion of police officers and still be murdered.

Just the thought made his blood run cold.

"What's going on?" she asked as he led the way to her office.

"I'm not sure."

"You must have some idea, or you wouldn't have called for the bomb detectors."

"I saw something attached to the Jeep's chassis. Looked like explosives, but I couldn't get a good enough view to be certain." He had gotten a clear enough glimpse to be worried, but he hadn't dared slide underneath to investigate further.

There were too many people on the street. Cars. Bicycles. Pedestrians on the sidewalk. If the Jeep exploded, it wasn't just the vehicle that would be taken out.

"Explosives? As in, a bomb?"

"I'm going to let the experts decide," he responded. King walked beside him, his scruff still up, his ears back. He may not have seen what was attached to the bottom of the Jeep, but he had smelled it.

And he hadn't liked it.

That was enough to concern Bradley.

His boss, Sergeant Gavin Sutherland, had agreed to bring his bomb-detecting dog, Tommy. He'd also said he would bring Detective Henry Roarke and his K-9 partner, Cody. Roarke was a former military explosives expert. Cody was a high-energy beagle with a nose for detecting bombs. If there was something there, Tommy and Cody would know it.

"Experts?" Sasha asked as they reached her office.

"Two of our bomb-detecting dogs are

the best in the business. If there are explosives around, they'll know it."

"And if there are?"

"We'll shut down the street and call in the bomb squad. The dogs and handlers should be here soon. I need you to wait in your office until I return for you."

"Which will be when?"

"Hopefully not long."

"That's vague."

"I wish I could offer a firmer timeline, but I can't. Sometimes the dogs locate a source quickly. Sometimes they take their time."

"If you'd like, I can call a cab and go to the hotel."

"Do you really think that's a safe idea? After everything that's happened already today?"

He thought she might be offended by the question, but she sighed. "You have a point. I'll wait in my office."

"No wandering the building? No heading out the back door to run errands?"

"Nope. I'll be sitting at my desk working on next weekend's show."

"You're sure?" he prodded, suddenly worried about leaving her.

"I'm sure."

"There's a lock on the door," he pointed out as he walked back into the hall. "Use it, okay?"

"Okay," she agreed, offering a quick smile.

She closed the door, and he waited until he heard the lock turn, then hurried outside. Gavin was already there, his vehicle parked in a no-parking zone a few feet away and angled purposely so that traffic had to take a wide path around. His boss stepped out of the vehicle when he saw Bradley.

Bradley liked and admired Gavin Sutherland. The dedicated cop had previously worked at the NYC K-9 Command Unit in Queens and had been promoted to sergeant of the Brooklyn K-9 Unit when the new team was formed back in the spring. If there was a bomb around, the

Sarge and Detective Henry Roarke were two hardworking cops you wanted working on the case.

"We're working to block traffic on both ends of the block," Gavin said. "Once we get a clearer picture of what's going on, we can make decisions about evacuating businesses."

"I'm not even sure it's a bomb, Sarge," Bradley said, giving King the down command as Gavin got Tommy out. The springer spaniel jumped down excitedly, prancing on his leash impatiently. Like all the dogs on the team, he loved his work and looked forward to doing the job he had been trained for.

"I'll walk him around your Jeep. See if he indicates. Looks like Henry is pulling up. Why don't you fill him in? Once I finish, he can bring Cody over."

Bradley nodded, leaving King where he was as he strode toward the marked K-9 vehicle pulling into a no-parking zone a few yards away. He waited as Henry exited the vehicle, watching as he opened the back hatch and allowed Cody to jump out. The beagle shook with excitement, his happy baying sounding over the roar of traffic.

He was ready to work and anxious to do it, but he'd have to wait his turn.

"How's it going?" Henry asked, his focus on the Jeep and Tommy.

"It'd be better if I hadn't had to call you and the sergeant out here."

"You really think someone planted a bomb under the Jeep?"

"I don't know, but I'm worried enough to call in the experts."

"Not experts. Just trained," Henry corrected with a clap on Bradley's back, following Sutherland and Tommy's progress around the Jeep.

Bradley would trust Henry Roarke with his life. A colleague and a friend, the former soldier knew exactly what it was like to be accused of a crime he hadn't committed. Earlier in the year, Henry had been investigated by Internal Affairs for "unlawful use of force" against an unarmed suspect. He'd been on desk duty for months, but the good news was that not only had he been fully vindicated, but he'd found love with the investigator on his case.

He and Henry walked around the front of the vehicle, Tommy dropping his head to sniff the bumper, the tires, behind the license plate. His tail was raised and his paws scrabbled at the pavement as he went to the driver's side of the vehicle.

"He's on to something," Henry said. "It's good you called us. You have an enemy gunning for you?"

"Just every criminal I ever locked up, but I think this has more to do with the shooting yesterday."

"And the note this morning? I was on a case this morning, but I heard about it."

Bradley nodded. "The victim's mother was murdered eighteen years ago and the shooter is a dead ringer for the killer."

"Relative?" he asked just as Tommy let out three quick barks. "He's found it. Guess it's Cody's turn."

He led Cody to the Jeep, gave him the command to find and followed along, leash in hand, as the beagle sniffed the underside of the Jeep, ran to the driver's side. Sniffed again. Howled.

"Same place," Gavin commented. "I'm going to block off the road and call in the bomb squad. In the meantime, let's start clearing the sidewalk. I know that you're off duty, but can you run caution tape to block the area? Backup will be here soon."

"No problem." He called for King to heel, then grabbed the caution tape from the sergeant's vehicle and used it to cordon off the sidewalk three hundred yards in every direction.

Sirens blared, police cruisers making their way to the scene. At the end of the block, the bomb squad van was trying to find a path through bumper-to-bumper traffic. The road was a mass of honking horns and curious onlookers. People darting across the road in front of vehicles that were attempting to get out the way of emergency vehicles.

It was a bad situation. One the perp might use to his advantage. Often criminals returned to the scene of the crime. It was possible Sasha's stalker was hiding in the crowd, watching the drama unfold.

Bradley glanced at the building where Sasha worked.

A few people stood in the doorway, watching as chaos erupted. Sasha wasn't there. She had said she'd be working behind the locked office door. He and King would do a quick circuit of the area, searching for a Martin Roker clone.

Not a twin. They knew Roker had no siblings. Hopefully the unit's excellent tech guru would get back to him soon with the information she'd dug up. If there was any.

Maybe someone who just happened to look similar to Martin Roker had become fixated on the case?

DNA from the note might lead to answers, but the lab was notoriously slow. Fortunately, Bradley had connections. Men and women at the lab who had known his adoptive parents, who knew his story and who were always eager to help when they could.

He pulled out his cell phone as he and King walked toward the crowd of by-standers, dialing the number for the lab as he scanned the faces. It didn't take him long to convince his adoptive father's old buddy to expedite the testing on the note.

Bradley needed to find the person who was stalking Sasha and get him off the street. Sasha had every right to live her life without fear. She should be free to walk to work and home, to take public transporta-tion, shop, move through her life without fear that she might be attacked.

Bradley would make certain she was.

He was as dedicated to that as he was to every case he worked, but he had to admit, there was something about Sasha that made him want to get more deeply involved. Her strength and courage, her determination to make a good life out of the tragedy of her past, were things he admired. He had lived through his own

tragedy. He knew how hard it was to overcome trauma, to work through grief and to
move on. Though he'd been long cleared
as a suspect in his parents' murders, a part
of him never forgot what it had felt like
to be accused, whispered about. To be
thought capable of something so heinous.
When the copycat murders occurred, rumors had run rampant, and he'd felt that
old shame and powerlessness that he had
felt when he was considered a suspect in
his parents' murders. Irrational as that
was. Bradley had worked hard to make a
name for himself in law enforcement. He
had established himself as someone with
integrity and honor.

But all the old pain and anger had risen
up in him at the double murder so eerily
similar to his parents'.

He'd been reminded of being the scared,
orphaned fourteen-year-old—and how
people couldn't be trusted, that no matter what he did, how much he had accomplished, he would always feel like the

teenager who was suspected in his parents' murders.

And his need to prove himself? It had never diminished. He wondered if that was what Sasha was trying to do with her feel-good stories and her cheerful on-air persona. Maybe she wanted to stop being the teenager who had lost her mother in a scandalous tragedy and prove herself as someone who found the good and right and wholesome in the world.

Whatever her motivation, the job had put her in the spotlight, and that might be the reason she had become the target of a lunatic.

Bradley scowled, making another circuit of the area as the bomb squad van finally arrived. The perp might be hiding in plain sight.

If he was, Bradley and King would find him.

SEVEN

Sasha wasn't sure how long she'd been working, but her neck hurt, her eyes burned and her stomach was growling.

She stood and stretched, glancing at the clock on the wall and frowning. It was after noon, the light filtering in through the window casting long shadows across the floor. She had silenced her phone, and she checked it, wondering if Bradley had left a message explaining why he hadn't returned.

No voice mail.

No message.

Nothing but glowing numbers announcing the time and reminding her that she hadn't eaten breakfast that morning. She had barely slept the night before. She was hungry. She was tired. She was finished with most of the prep work for next week's story.

Any other day, she would have turned off her computer, grabbed her coat and headed home. This wasn't any other day. Bradley was worried someone had planted a bomb under his Jeep, and she was waiting to be told it was safe to leave the building.

She did a quick scan of local news and found a blurb about the bomb squad being on scene near Ocean Avenue. There was a picture of her building and the black bomb squad van. No information about what had been found.

If anything had.

She rubbed the back of her neck and opened the file cabinet closest to the window. Her emergency supply of chocolate and energy bars was depleted. There was a chocolate protein shake. She shook it half-heartedly as she paced to the door.

The building seemed unnaturally quiet. No voices. No footsteps. No buzz of activity as the evening broadcasting crew arrived to begin prepping.

Had the police shut down the building?

She tried calling Prudence, but it went straight to voice mail. Bradley's phone did the same.

She unlocked the door, peering out into the hallway.

The studio light was green. Nothing was being broadcast.

From what she could see, the room was empty.

"Anyone around?" she called, leaning out of her office. She didn't want to take chances, but she didn't like the idea that she might be in the building alone, that the police might have evacuated the entire area, and she could be the only person left within blast distance of the bomb.

"Bradley would have called you," she reminded herself. "Even if he forgot, Prudence certainly wouldn't leave you behind if the place was evacuated."

Not if she knew Sasha was there.

Most days, Sasha left the door to her

office open, the tiny space making her feel claustrophobic when it was closed. If Prudence had walked past on her way out of the building, she would have assumed Sasha had left for the day.

"You're being ridiculous," Sasha murmured, but she couldn't shake the feeling that she had been abandoned, and that the best thing she could do was leave as quickly as possible.

She closed the office door and moved down the hall, nearly running as she passed one closed door after another. As she'd suspected, the offices were empty, the normal daytime crew gone.

She grabbed her coat as she flew through the reception area, shrugging into it and stepping into the silent corridor. She hurried toward the stairs, certain she heard voices somewhere below. She relaxed a little, slowing her pace, telling herself there was nothing to be afraid of.

She passed a small alcove where two chairs and a table sat. A good place to eat lunch when it was too rainy to go outside, it wasn't usually empty at this time of day. Still, she was surprised to see a man, his back to her, standing in front of the window. Not something alarming or even worth noting.

Until he turned and moved toward her. Quickly. Decisively. Hand clamping over her mouth as he pulled her into his chest.

She saw his face.

Just briefly.

Just enough to know that her worst fears were coming true. Martin Roker. Whispering in her ear.

"I've been waiting for you, Sasha."

She tried to slam her head into his chin, but his grip on her tightened, the hand he'd slammed over her mouth pressing so hard that she bit the inside of her lip and tasted blood.

"None of that, okay?" His breath was a fetid mixture of alcohol and tobacco, his palm sweaty and cold. She gagged.

He shook her. Hard.

"You'd better get yourself together, or

you won't live long enough to see tomorrow. Understood?"

She nodded.

"Good. Good. This wasn't what I planned, but we're going to make it work, right?"

She didn't respond as he pushed her back through the corridor, away from the stairs and the voices.

"Good thing I'm good at improvising. Those explosives were a stroke of genius. Perfect distraction for the cops, the dogs and everyone in this building. People are so predictable, gawking at the misfortunes of others while they whine about their own."

She wasn't sure if he was talking to himself or to her.

His grip shifted from her mouth to her throat, his hand pressing against her windpipe and jugular as he pushed her through the hallway, one hand wrapped around her torso, holding her arms down tight to her sides.

She couldn't breathe.

Could barely think.

She wanted to scream, but there wasn't enough air for that. Not enough energy in her body to fight. Her legs went weak, and she would have collapsed if he hadn't been holding her waist so tightly.

"Walk!" he growled.

"I can't breathe," she managed to choke out.

"As if I care," he responded, but he shifted his palm, his fingers sliding into her hair and fisting there.

She took a deep breath, ignoring the burning pain of her hair being pulled from her head. She didn't care if she went bald. As long as she could breathe.

They reached the end of the hall and turned left, moving into a narrow corridor that led to the building's only elevator. An emergency exit was there, too. Just a few short steps away.

If she could get there and push open the door, an alarm would sound. Help would come.

She hoped.

Please, God, she prayed silently. *Give me an opportunity to escape.*

She imagined her mother had done the same when she had seen Martin Roker pointing a gun at her across the parking lot. Sasha had tried, over the years, to block those thoughts from her head, to not think about the last moments of her mother's life, to not contemplate the terror she must have felt, the desperation to survive.

Now she couldn't stop thinking about it.

She couldn't stop wondering if her mother had turned and run or tried to reason with her killer. There had been witness statements given to the police, shocked coworkers who had given hints of what had happened.

Martin calling her mother's name.

Her mother turning.

A shot ringing out.

Sasha steeled herself as her attacker tried to press the elevator call button with his elbow.

He cursed under his breath and tried again without success.

"Push the button!" he demanded. "Now!"

She almost did, her arm twitching and then falling to her side.

"I can't," she lied. "You're holding my arms too tightly."

He cursed again, loosening the arm that held hers down. Not completely. But enough.

"Push it!" he nearly screamed.

She jabbed at the button, then shoved backward and slammed him into the wall. The thud seemed to shake the floor.

His arms fell away, and she ran to the exit, slamming her palm against the bar that opened the door, stumbling through as a siren shrieked and he snagged her coat.

She teetered on the metal landing of an exterior fire escape, her heels stuck through holes that allowed rain to drain through the floor.

She kicked out of them, throwing off her coat and whirling around, slamming both arms into Roker's chest. He stumbled back. She tried to run, but he snagged her ankle, pulling her leg out from under her. Her chin hit the metal railing, and she saw stars, tasted more blood.

She didn't have time to think about it.

Didn't have time for anything but action.

She kicked hard, slamming her foot into Roker's head and scrambling away, the siren still screaming. A dog barked. A man called out.

Roker was gone, metal clanging and shaking as he ran up the fire escape.

Bradley pulled his firearm as he and King ran up the fire escape. He didn't dare shoot. Not with Sasha between him and the perp. His heart raced as he watched a blond-haired thin man sprint up the fire escape, step onto the roof and disappear from view. He couldn't see a face or features, but the build, hair and height seemed to be the same as the guy who had fired into the diner.

The Martin Roker look-alike had been

inside the building while they were out disarming the bomb he'd planted. The fact that Bradley had allowed himself to be distracted was infuriating. He knew what people were capable of. He understood how dangerous the world could be.

His mistake could have cost Sasha her life.

She lay still on the second-floor landing, her stockinged feet hanging over the edge of the first step.

Had she been injured?

Worse?

King reached her side and darted past, his desire to apprehend the suspect superseding everything else.

He bounded up to the next landing, heading toward the roof.

Bradley didn't dare let him go farther. Not with other officers and security personnel racing through the building and heading up to the roof. Anyone on the move would be King's target.

"Cease," he yelled as the Malinois jumped onto the roof.

No fear. No worry. No concern for the three-story drop.

As if a switch had been flicked off, King stopped.

"Come!"

King reluctantly returned to the fire escape and headed back down the stairs.

Bradley got to Sasha's side and reached for her neck, his fingers brushing over warm flesh as he searched for her pulse.

"My heart is beating just fine," she muttered, flipping onto her back and looking into his eyes. There was blood dripping from a deep cut on her chin, but she looked more angry than hurt, her eyes flashing. She sat up.

"Not too fast," he said, putting a hand on her shoulder to make certain she didn't topple over.

"If I fall over and give myself another gash in the face, it will be my fault. I can't believe I did something so stupid." She grabbed her coat and pressed it against her chin. "I'm sorry about this, Bradley."

"Why should you apologize because a lunatic is hunting you?"

"Because if I'd stayed in my office like you'd asked me to, he wouldn't have had a chance to grab me," she responded, using his shoulder to push herself to her feet.

She seemed steady enough, her bloodied, bruised knees flashing through holes in her stockings.

"I should have called and let you know what was going on," he replied, impressed by her willingness to own her mistakes.

"You can fill me in after you get that guy," she replied, pointing to the roof. "He can't have gone far."

He didn't tell her that he could have gone any number of places—back inside the building, down another fire escape, onto another roof. The buildings in this neighborhood were close enough together that someone brave or foolish enough might make the leap.

"You guys okay up there?" Henry called, Cody baying excitedly as they both headed up the stairs.

"She needs an ambulance," Bradley replied.

"What she needs is for you to stop hovering over her and go chase the perp," Sasha corrected.

"I'm glad to see that the knock on your head didn't damage your ability to argue," he said, smiling as she scowled.

"I'm not arguing. I'm simply pointing out that, while you are standing here babysitting me, the guy who fired the shot into the diner and planted a bomb under your Jeep is escaping."

"We've got officers heading up to the roof, ma'am," Henry said as he reached the landing. "Once the alarm sounded, we figured the perp might be trying to make his way out of the building without being spotted."

"He's escaped before," Sasha pointed out, pulling the coat away and probing the still-bleeding wound. "Doesn't feel like it needs stitches. Maybe some superglue. I've got some at home."

"Superglue?" Bradley asked, leaning in for a closer look.

"Sure. That's what I did when I was a kid and my father was working. If I cut myself, I'd clean it out and glue the wound shut. Works like a charm."

Henry snorted. "I'm heading up to the roof. Don't forget, McGregor. You're off duty."

He didn't need the reminder.

He was very aware that he and King were sidelined. There were plenty of K-9 teams and police officers who could give chase, but he could admit he wanted in on it. He wanted to find the guy who had hurt Sasha, and he wanted to make him pay.

He frowned as he watched Henry and Cody race up the fire escape.

"You're upset," Sasha commented.

"Frustrated."

"Because?"

"King is one of the best apprehension dogs in the nation. It would be great if we could go after this guy."

"You really don't have to stay with me,

Detective," she said, glancing down at the crowd of EMS personnel gathering in the alley below them. "There are plenty of people to keep an eye on me until you get back."

"That's not the way things work. I'm off duty. When I'm off duty, King and I don't get to chase bad guys."

"Then what do you get to do?"

"Chase seagulls, Frisbees and squirrels. Turn the local dog park into a dog wrestling ground. Laundry."

She laughed, wincing as she pressed the coat to her chin again. "Aside from the laundry, that sounds like a fun day."

"You think so?"

"Of course. Who doesn't love chasing seagulls, Frisbees and squirrels?" Her eyes were deep amber in the sunlight, her lashes thick and dark. She had a few freckles on her nose and cheeks that stood in stark contrast to her pale skin.

"Do you need to sit down?" he asked, alarmed by her pallor.

"No. I need to get myself cleaned up and

get to police headquarters. I want to give my statement and look at the lineup."

"That can wait, Sasha."

"Until?" she asked, taking a step down and then another.

"You're feeling better."

"You know what will make me feel better, Detective? Figuring out what all this is about, knowing the guy who's been stalking me has been caught and is behind bars, moving on with my life." Her voice shook, and he touched her shoulder as he followed her down the stairs. Close enough to catch her if she fell. Far enough away that she might not realize he was hovering.

"It's going to be okay," he said.

"Of course it will be," she responded. "It's always okay eventually, but for right now, it isn't. For right now, I need answers."

"I understand."

"Do you?" she asked, as she reached the first-floor landing. Several EMTs were rolling a gurney through the alley, the wheels bouncing over holes in the asphalt.

"Yes. Are you familiar with the Emery murders?"

"Who in Sheepshead Bay isn't?"

"You probably also know there were a lot of similarities between that double homicide and my parents' murders. Until we figure out who killed the Emerys and why, I'm not going to be able to rest."

"Your K-9 unit caught your parents' murderer last month, didn't they? And everyone seems to think the Emerys' killer was a copycat."

He nodded. "I was cleared of being a suspect in my parents' murders a long time ago, Sasha. But the murders of the Emerys brought it all back for me for exactly that reason—a copycat. Sometimes, late at night, I wonder if people are thinking, 'Hey, maybe it was Bradley McGregor wearing that clown mask this time around, getting revenge on another neglectful set of parents, getting revenge for being considered a suspect when he wasn't the killer.'"

"Oh, no, Bradley. That's awful. No one thinks that."

He shrugged. "Probably not. But that's what goes through my mind in the middle of the night when I can't sleep. I need to catch the Emerys' killer so that I can finally move on."

"I'm sorry you're going through this," she said, her eyes filled with sympathy that he hadn't expected.

He was used to people assuming that his childhood and his life had made him tough. He cultivated a gruff persona that convinced people he wasn't easily hurt, but that was because he had been hurt. It was because the wounds were still there, open and raw. Never healing because the gossip and whispers had never stopped in his own head. No matter how hard he had worked or how upright a life he lived, he couldn't stop thinking that some people were going to believe he was cut from the same cloth as his parents. He wished he could let it all go. Wished he could believe it when his colleagues told him how respected he was in the community, in the K-9 unit itself.

"I didn't tell you so you would be sorry," he said gruffly. "I told you because I want you to know that I understand how much of a hold the past has. I know what it's like to want answers. To *need* them."

She reached street level, stepped off the fire escape and turned to face him as EMTs swarmed around her. "I'll help you find what you're looking for," she said.

He had no idea what she meant and no chance to say that every officer on the K-9 unit had been helping him for seven months. The EMTs began looking at her cut, asking her questions, getting medical information that they were relaying to the hospital.

He wanted to stay behind and wait for news about the perp's apprehension.

Or his escape.

He also wanted to stick close to Sasha's side.

He liked her positive attitude, her determination, her drive. And he wanted to know more about her life, her job, her friends and hobbies. She interested him in a way few women had in the past decade. He'd spent years pursuing his career as he helped raise his sister. Their adoptive parents had been in their sixties when she graduated from high school. Joe and Allison Brady had given everything they had to make certain Bradley and Penny had the love and support they needed. They had died within weeks of each other—Allison from cancer, Joe from a heart attack. Losing them had left a gaping hole that Bradley had spent the past four years trying to fill. He had supported Penny as she finished her education, encouraged her as she pursued her career. He had given her a place to live rent free, and he had enjoyed her company, enjoyed knowing she was safe in bed at night.

He hadn't had time for more than that. Not with his hectic workload. But Penny would be getting married soon. She'd move out and create a whole new life for herself. It was what Bradley had been wanting, what he had been praying for—that she would have whatever life she wanted.

He was happy for her. Happy for himself, too. He had accomplished what he had promised he would when his parents had come home from the hospital with a tiny little girl wrapped in one of his old blankets. He had known then that he would have to protect her, care for her and give her what he knew their parents wouldn't. He had promised himself that he would make sure she grew up, got her education and had a better life than the one she had been born into.

Done, done and done.

Now he could focus on pursuing his dreams.

Whatever they might be.

Work, sure.

He'd known from the day he had been cleared of his parents' murders that he would go into law enforcement.

But there were other things he'd dreamed of while he was a young beat cop working his way up the ranks. Friendship. Love. Someone to go home to at night.

Maybe that was why he noticed how attractive and intelligent Sasha was. Maybe his subconscious mind was reminding him that he had a life to live, too. At thirty-four, it wasn't too late to achieve the life he had put on hold while his sister pursued her education and established herself as a vital part of the K-9 unit.

He followed the EMTs as they escorted Sasha to the ambulance.

He could hear her soft voice through the more strident tones of the men and women who were treating her.

"Seriously, just hand me some superglue and let me be on my way," she said.

He smiled as one of the EMTs explained that the cut was going to require more than a couple of dabs of glue.

"Then just bandage me up. I have places to be."

Bradley's grin widened as he jostled his way through what seemed like an army of medical professionals.

"Tell them, Detective," she said as she caught sight of him. He thought she might have smiled, but it was hard to see through the gauze bandage that was wrapped around the lower part of her face.

"If King can ride along, we'll escort you to the hospital and then to headquarters once you're stitched up," he replied.

"That wasn't what I was hoping you'd say," she muttered, but she seemed to give in to the inevitable, allowing herself to be helped onto the back of the ambulance.

He flashed his badge at one of the EMTs. "Mind if my partner and I ride along?"

"Not a problem, as long as he isn't planning on taking a chunk out of the crew."

"He's too well trained for that," he responded, jumping on board. King followed, sitting down beside him, his head on his paws, his expressive eyes conveying just how disgusted he was with the turn of events.

"Sorry, buddy," Bradley said. "I'll make this up to you tomorrow."

"With a trip to the beach to chase

gulls?" Sasha asked, leaning her head back against the side of the ambulance and closing her eyes.

"That and a trip to the dog park," he responded. "If you're up to it, maybe you'd like to join us." The invitation slipped out, and her eyes flew open.

"So you can keep an eye on me?" she asked.

It would have been easy to agree, to let her think he wasn't thinking about other things—like getting to know her, spending time with her, enjoying a relaxing afternoon with someone who didn't seem to have any agenda except kindness.

"What would you say if I said there were other reasons?" he responded, because he believed in shooting straight and speaking plainly.

She eyed him for a moment, the white gauze making her expression difficult to read.

Finally, she nodded.

"You know what? I'd like that," she said,

and he was surprised at just how happy that made him.

"Me, too," he said as the ambulance lurched forward and headed to the hospital.

EIGHT

The cut on her chin hadn't been nearly
as bad as everyone had seemed to think
it was. The doctor at the emergency room
had cleaned it, glued it and pressed a
gauze bandage over the area.

Nothing she couldn't have done herself.

She fingered the bandage as she paced
her hotel room. Bradley had escorted her
there after she had given her statement
and chosen Martin Roker from a picture
lineup—with the added explanation that
the man stalking her had been a carbon
copy, not Martin Roker himself, of course.
Bradley had insisted on walking her to
her room and checking every corner of it.
Then he had stood on the threshold, his
jaw dark with a five-o'clock shadow, his

eyes red-rimmed with fatigue, and made her promise to stay locked inside until he returned the following afternoon.

For their...

Appointment?

Meeting?

Date?

She shied away from the last word, refusing to acknowledge it. She didn't date. Michael had cured her of the desire for male companionship.

At least, that was what she always told herself.

Her college sweetheart, Michael had been exactly the man she had thought she wanted in her life—charismatic and charming, caring and compassionate. His faith had seemed stronger than hers, his understanding of the Bible impressive. He had taught men's Bible studies at college and been a youth leader at his church.

She had fallen for him quickly when they'd met at church during her sophomore year. He'd been a law student, getting ready to take the bar. She'd been studying communications, hoping for a career in journalism. He had swept her off her feet with phone calls and flowers and little notes to tell her he was thinking about her.

It had felt like the real deal, the happily-ever-after.

They'd married two days after she'd graduated. He had passed the bar the following week. On paper, they worked. A power couple ready to make a difference in the world. She had adored him, and she had thought he'd felt the same about her.

She had been wrong.

He had cheated on her twice during their short marriage. She had forgiven him the first time. The second time, he had chosen to walk away. Five years of marriage, and he'd fallen in love with someone more exciting, more interesting, more passionate. At least, that was the way he'd described it. Sasha figured he had simply gotten bored with his straitlaced life. He had walked away from the Bible studies and joined a fitness club. He had traded

Bible quotes in for inspirational speeches. He practiced law, but his real passion was encouraging people to live their best lives, and his best life had not included staying with someone who believed in traditional marriage and traditional values.

Boring.

Michael had used the word over and over again as he had explained why he was packing his bags and filing for divorce.

She had wanted to deny it, but there had been a small part of her that had thought he might be right. She had been in her twenties and working hard to balance being married with building her career.

Working long hours, returning home to spend frantic minutes tossing together a meal she and Michael could eat together. Wearing flannel pajamas to bed. Throwing her hair up into a ponytail every day. Her mother's murder had taught her that life could be unpredictable, and she had made it a habit to do everything she could to protect herself from the unexpected.

Maybe her marriage had died because of it.

Or maybe Michael was just a lying, cheating jerk.

She frowned, the skin on her chin pulling painfully.

She walked to the mirror and pulled off the bandage.

The cut was on the underside of her chin, the skin around it bruised and swollen. She had nearly died a few hours ago. One misstep and she would have.

She touched a dark smudge on her cheek. A fingertip-sized mark that had probably been made when Roker dug his hand into her face to keep her from screaming.

There were several more on her neck.

She'd changed into pajamas after Bradley left, and her pale legs peeked out from beneath the hem of oversize sleep shorts. Her knees were raw and bruised, but she was here. She was breathing. She had more time to pursue the plans God had for her.

Whatever they might be.

She sighed, dropping into a chair and grabbing her laptop from the desk. She typed in her password, typed the name Emery into the search bar and watched as hundreds of articles popped up. Sheepshead Bay had been consumed by the story, caught up in the way history had repeated itself.

A copycat murder twenty years to the date the McGregors had been killed. A young survivor the sole witness. Not enough physical evidence to pin the crime on anyone. Like everyone else in the area, Sasha was familiar with the case. She knew the Brooklyn K-9 Unit had been working tirelessly to apprehend the person responsible.

Her job required her to search for good-news stories.

This certainly wasn't one. Lucy Emery had been neglected by her parents. There were a few articles about neighbors who'd seen the little girl playing alone in the front yard at just three years old. People coming and going from the two-family house. The litter that cluttered the yard. The broken toys she was often seen playing with.

Sasha could recall reading that Lucy's aunt Willow, her father's sister, had constantly tried to intervene and was constantly turned away by her brother and sister-in-law. In fact, the day of the murders, Willow had gone over to the home to give the Emerys an ultimatum about Lucy and the lack of care. She'd found her brother and sister-in-law dead. Her niece crying and alone. Now Willow and her husband, another detective on the K-9 team, were raising Lucy in a safe, loving home.

Sasha skimmed several articles, jotting notes and making a list of neighbors who had been willing to talk to the press. She knew the neighborhood. She'd covered several feel-good stories there, highlighting the good that came out of poverty and struggle. Maybe people would be willing to tell her things that they hadn't wanted to say to the police. She knew from news conferences that local authorities were searching for someone named Andy. Someone that Lucy Emery insisted was her friend, and who the police wanted to speak to regarding the Emery murders.

If Andy was a friend of Lucy's parents, perhaps he or she knew something that would lead investigators to the murderer. Sasha had no intention of sticking her nose in where it wasn't wanted, but she didn't see any reason to not visit the neighborhood, take a few pictures of the crime scene and see if any of the neighbors were willing to talk to her.

She could do a story on it. A switch from her normal, but still with a happy ending. A neglected child finding love and security after her parents' deaths.

It was a story that had played out before.

One she had been fascinated with since she had heard about the seeming connection between the Emery and McGregor murders. Bradley and Penelope McGregor could have chosen to go down the path their parents had taken. Both had been neglected. Bradley had been his sister's primary caregiver during the years their parents were alive. When they died, he had been accused of the murders, brought in for questioning, been found guilty in the court of public opinion.

And still, somehow, he had found a way out of what he had been born into. He had focused his energy on justice. He had pursued law enforcement the way other people might have pursued drugs or alcohol or crime.

She was fascinated by that, curious about the spirit that had driven him, the people who had stood behind him, the strength of character that had sustained him when his entire world had crumbled.

Maybe that was why she wanted to help him find the Emerys' killer. She wanted him to have closure so that he could move on without wondering if there were whispered accusations following him. Granted, all that was lodged in his gut. But she understood.

That wasn't why she had agreed to go

to the beach with him and King, though. Yes, it would be an outing, not focused on work, where she would be safe in the presence of an armed detective.

The real reason: she liked Bradley.

She was interested in learning more about him.

Not for the cable show. For herself.

"There," she said, setting her laptop on the table and crossing the room. She pulled back the curtain that covered the window and stared into the dark night. "You admitted you like him. Was that so hard?"

Not as hard as having another broken heart would be.

Just take it one day at a time. See about the business of living today before you worry about what might come tomorrow.

That was what her father would say to her if he was around.

It was good advice, but harder to live than she wanted to admit. She liked to have a plan. She liked to know what was coming next. The unknown scared her.

And relationships?

They were filled with unknowns and dark corners and unexpected twists and turns.

Her cell phone rang, and she jumped, nearly tumbling in her haste to grab it from the charging port. "Hello," she said breathlessly.

"Sasha? It's Bradley. Is everything all right?"

"Fine," she managed to say, her foolish heart jumping with joy at the sound of his voice.

"You sure? You sound out of breath."

"The phone startled me."

"Still on edge after the incident at work?" he asked, his voice warm with concern.

"A little. Do you have news?"

"Not as much as we'd like. After the bomb squad disarmed the bomb, the evidence team was able to get a fingerprint off the adhesive that was used to stick it to the underside of my Jeep."

"Any matches in the data bank?"

"Unfortunately, no, but I put a call in to the DNA lab. I have a friend there who is expediting the test on the blood we found on the note."

"Do you really think it belongs to the perpetrator?" she asked. "He isn't stupid, and leaving DNA evidence is."

"He's smart enough to be cocky. Or thinks he is. Perps like that make plenty of mistakes, because they think they are too smart to get caught."

"I hope you're right. I hope it's his, and I hope there's a match in the system."

"Even if there isn't, we may be able to find him. Our tech guru is looking for family connections to Martin Roker. And there are ancestry registries online that give people an opportunity to connect with long-lost family members. One of our officers knows how to run DNA through the system to look for family matches. I also asked the local police station that handled your mother's case if there was anything left in connection."

"It's a closed file. Why would they keep evidence?"

"An officer-involved shooting is a big deal. Sometimes family shows up years later and claims undue force."

"It's been eighteen years."

"Right. I wasn't sure there would be anything," he said. She heard people talking in the background. Phones ringing.

"Are you still at the office?" she asked.

"Yes. The team is meeting in a few minutes. I wanted to call you before then."

"It's your day off."

"I'm not sure I know what that means," he said with a quiet chuckle. "Regarding the evidence in your mom's murder investigation, the handgun Roker used was in the box, along with his wallet and gloves he wore when he committed the crime. I had the evidence team swab for DNA, and I sent that and the gloves to the lab. Just in case the person who is after you is related."

"For someone who has a day off, you are certainly working hard."

"I want this guy behind bars. The sooner it happens, the happier I'll be. You're still in your room?"

"Locked in and not going anywhere."

"Good. I'd worry about you if I thought you were wandering around without protection. My meeting is about to start. Try to get some rest, Sasha. I'll check in before I leave tonight and call after my shift tomorrow to see if there's anything you want me to bring when I pick you up."

"Talk to you later," she said, not wanting the call to end.

But he disconnected, and she set the phone back in the port, her stomach doing a crazy little flip of excitement. Bradley wasn't trying to be charming. He didn't seem to want to impress or disarm her. He was doing his job the way he always did and taking the time to update her on the steps he was taking to find her stalker.

It was what she imagined he would do for the victim of any crime. She couldn't see him changing his routine to impress a woman or trying harder because he wanted to seem more driven or more interesting. From what she had seen, Bradley was exactly who he seemed—a focused police detective who gave everything he had to the job.

She found that very attractive and very intriguing.

That scared her, but not enough to make her back out of tomorrow's beach run.

She grabbed her computer and settled into the chair again.

Warm, fuzzy feelings were great, but until her stalker was behind bars and the Emery murders had been solved, there wouldn't be anything else. There couldn't be. They were both too focused and intent to veer from the course set in front of them.

Meetings were about as much fun as root canals.

And usually took three times longer.

The entire team had gathered, some of them with their dogs. Some alone. King was under Bradley's chair, huffing quietly every few minutes. Obviously miffed about the long day indoors.

Bradley shifted in his seat, the pad of paper in front of him covered in notes about Sasha's case and about the Emery murders. Since the arrest of Randall Gage, the man who had murdered Bradley's parents, the Emery case had grown too cold for his liking. The newest information they had was from Gage, and it hadn't helped much. Detective Tyler Walker, Bradley's future brother-in-law, had gone to see Randall Gage in prison and had asked for help—his take on why the copycat killer had acted. Gage had said that they needed to look for someone the Emerys had wronged. Maybe a drug deal gone bad. Money owed. Something that made the need for revenge or repayment paramount. He had also claimed that if the killer had seen Lucy Emery being neglected the way he had seen Penelope McGregor being neglected, he had probably figured they deserved everything they got. Children deserved better than parents like that, and Randall Gage seemed to think he and the Emerys' murderer had done the world a favor. He also thought that if the police wanted to find the killer, they needed to find someone who knew the family well, someone who knew Lucy well.

"That brings us back to Andy," Bradley said.

Gavin looked up from notes he was reading through. "What does?"

"The information Tyler got from Randall Gage. If he's right, we need to find someone who was close enough to Lucy Emery to care that her parents were neglecting her. Someone who might have used that as a secondary reason to murder them."

"Right. If we find Andy, I think we may just find the perp," Tyler agreed from his place across the table.

Someone knocked on the door to the conference room. It swung open, and his sister walked in, a large box of carryout coffee in one hand and a stack of disposable cups in the other. Anyone looking at him and Penny would know they were siblings. They were both tall, and though Penny's hair was red and his was more auburn, they had the same dark brown eyes.

"Don't expect this every time," she announced with a grin as she set everything on the conference table. "I have more important things to do with my time than keep you all awake."

She glanced at Tyler, a soft smile on her face.

They made a good couple.

That didn't mean Bradley hadn't warned his future brother-in-law about the consequences of hurting his sister.

"Thanks, Penny," Bradley said, and she turned her smile in his direction.

"No problem. I'm heading home. I'll see you when you get there." She bustled out of the room. Quick. Efficient. Cheerful. The K-9 unit wouldn't function as effectively without her. Bradley hated the flashes of memory that would overtake him at the most random times. His sister being hunted by Randall Gage last month, determined to "get rid of the witness" he'd left behind twenty years ago. With Gage awaiting trial and sure to go down for a long time, Penny would be safe. Especially married to a detective Bradley knew well and trusted.

Bradley was proud of his sister, proud of what his Penny was accomplishing, the reputation she had built for herself in the short time she had been there. She'd survived so much and was stronger for it. He hoped Penny knew how much he admired her. He had a feeling she did.

For a few moments, the group chatted as coffee was poured and cups passed around. Bradley sipped his, ignoring King's impatient nudge.

"I think we should go back to the Emerys' neighbors," Henry said, drawing everyone's focus back to the case. "Ask around again. Someone has to know Andy. Someone who wasn't comfortable saying so before. Who knows—maybe this Andy guy got to the neighbors and threatened them when we first started coming around asking about him."

"We've been through that neighborhood dozens of times," Jackson Davison pointed out. "But if it'll help, I don't mind asking around again. Maybe a new face will bring new answers."

"We can only hope," Gavin responded with a tired sigh. "This case is dragging on, and the media is still having a heyday with it. Hopefully Ms. Eastman isn't going to do a show on it."

"Sasha Eastman?" Officer Vivienne Armstrong asked. "From that cable television show? Good news only, or something like that. What's she have to do with the Emery case?"

"She was here last week, hoping to get an interview with Penny and Bradley," Tyler said, an edge of disgust in his voice. "Now she's claiming that a stalker is after her."

"She's not claiming," Bradley cut in. "A stalker *is* after her. I saw the guy going after her today at her office building. He's the same person who planted explosives under my Jeep. And the one who shot at her the other day."

"Her mother was murdered eighteen years ago," Gavin said. "Whoever is after her seems to have a connection to that. Any news on the DNA evidence, Bradley? You said you asked to have it expedited?"

"Right. They can usually move it through quickly. My friend at the lab said they might have something for us by the early a.m. And Eden is checking deeper into Roker's past."

Tyler nodded, stifling a yawn before taking a quick sip of coffee. Everyone was running on fumes, but adrenaline and the call for justice kept them all going. "I may have needed this more than I thought."

"We've covered everything pressing," the sergeant said. "If you want to visit the Emerys' neighborhood, I'd appreciate it, Jackson. I'm ready to close this case."

"No problem. I'll head out there during my shift Sunday. See what I can dig up."

"Good. Let's set another meeting for a

couple days from now. Hopefully by then we'll have more answers than questions." Gavin stood, the rest of the team following suit. The group filed out, officers, dogs, the quiet murmur of voices and rustle of K-9 fur a familiar and comforting melody.

Law enforcement had been Bradley's life for more than a decade. He enjoyed what he did. If pressed, he told people he felt called to it.

But there was more to life.

The members of the K-9 unit seemed to have been discovering that over the past few months. One by one, they had found love, and he had watched with shock and amusement as they had fallen hard and fast.

The romances had begun back in April, when his friend and colleague Detective Nate Slater answered a homicide call at the Emery house and met newly orphaned Lucy and her aunt Willow. The tragic case had brought them together, and now Lucy was safe and well cared for, Nate's K-9 partner, Murphy, a gentle yellow Lab, the little girl's extra protector.

Bradley glanced over at narcotics officer Raymond Morrow, who'd been reunited with an old flame when a dangerous drug dealer had come after Karenna Pressley. Ray sure was happier these days. As was Officer Belle Montera, her German shepherd partner, Justice, walking beside her to her desk. Belle had had the difficult task of convincing a known relative of Randall Gage to give up his family member for the sake of justice. Thanks to the efforts of both Belle and US marshal Emmett Gage, the killer of his and Penny's parents was behind bars and facing trial.

Detective Henry Roarke's K-9 partner, Cody, a cute beagle, let out a little bay. Everyone glanced over as Henry gave Cody his favorite new toy to play with beside his chair. Bradley had been worried for Henry for a while when he'd been under investigation by IA, but he and investigator Olivia Vance were now planning a wedding. Officer Vivienne Armstrong passed by Henry's chair with her own K-9 partner, Hank, a black-and-white border collie, grinning at Cody, who was enjoying his stuffed moose. Vivienne was now engaged to Caleb Black, the FBI agent who'd been on Randall Gage's trail. Then there was Officer Jackson Davison, who'd managed the impossible: convincing forensic scientist Darcy Fields to give up her rule against dating cops for him.

Of all the new couples among his friends and coworkers in the K-9 unit, the one that brought him some measure of peace, allowed him to get a little more sleep at night, was Penny and Tyler. With Randall Gage in prison, Penny was safe—and always would be with Tyler by her side.

Lots of happy couples. As for Bradley, he figured his path was already written in stone. When Penny had admitted her love for Tyler, he had been happy for her, but there had been a hint of something beneath the surface of that. Emptiness. Longing. The sickening feeling that life was passing, and he had devoted himself to something that would never devote it-self to him.

Law enforcement was his calling, but one day he would retire. He and his K-9 partner would spend their days on the beach or exploring parks. Maybe he would have nieces and nephews. Obviously, he would have friends, but there was loneli-ness in the thought of growing old without someone to talk to late at night or wake up with in the morning.

Years ago, he had made the decision to devote himself to his sister, to make cer-tain she had the happiest, most stable up-bringing possible. Once she was grown, he had put the extra energy and time into his job, telling himself that romance and relationships were for men who weren't committed to justice the way he was.

That used to satisfy him.

Lately, though, those reasons didn't seem strong enough to make him spend the rest of his life alone.

"Come on, King," he said, suddenly exhausted and ready to put the day behind him. Hopefully by the time he arrived home, he'd be ready to take King for a run. Even at this time of the night, the Malinois needed to expend energy. First, though, he'd check in on Sasha, even though it was late. He'd been busy tonight, but she'd been front and center in his thoughts. He knew she was safe at the hotel, that she'd call him if she needed him. But he wanted to hear her voice.

That was unnerving.

He pressed in her number, relieved when she answered right away. She sounded tired.

"Everything okay?" he asked.

"Yup," she said. "Thanks for checking in. But I'm locked in, no trouble here all night." She let out a little yawn. "I'm ready to turn in. See you tomorrow, Bradley."

He was looking forward to just that a little too much. "See you tomorrow," he said, disconnecting and putting his phone in his pocket, Sasha's face, her voice, lingering in his mind.

The streets were nearly empty as he

drove home. He didn't bother sitting down, just changed into running gear and headed out into the night. Chilly November air stung his cheeks as he and King did their normal three-mile loop. When they finished, he walked King to a small park and allowed him to sniff bushes and rocks before they returned home.

It was nearly two by the time they returned home. King was finally content, his tail wagging happily as he sprang onto Bradley's bed and settled down for the night.

Trying to be as quiet as possible so he didn't wake up Penny, who was asleep in the bedroom across the hall, Bradley showered quickly, anxious to get a few hours of sleep before the alarm went off and he had to get ready for work again.

He'd barely laid his head on the pillow when his phone rang, the shrill sound making King raise his head and huff softly.

Bradley grabbed the phone from the nightstand. "Hello?"

"Bradley? It's Mitch from the lab."

"You're working late," he said, suddenly wide-awake.

"We have a lot piled up, and I wanted to prioritize yours. We pulled DNA from the sample you sent. Male. European ancestry. No match in the criminal database that I can find."

"You already ran it? You've gone above and beyond, Mitch."

"Just doing my job and helping out a friend. I've sent you an email with information that you can use to find connections in public ancestry searches, but, to be honest, I got curious and ran it through a few myself."

"You're not calling because there wasn't a match," Bradley said, flipping on the light and grabbing a paper and pen from his desk drawer.

"You know me well," Mitch chuckled. "Okay. Here's what I've got. The DNA donor is related to Wanda Anderson."

"Not a name I'm familiar with."

"Would you be if I told you she'd once

filed a restraining order against Martin Roker? I called Eden Chang and asked her to look into that connection, and guess what?"

His heart skipped a beat, and he scribbled the name, his mind racing with possibilities.

"The restraining order was a domestic violence situation," Mitch continued. "Wanda had been in a relationship with Martin. And since the donor is a close family relative of hers, Eden did some digging. Wanda had a child out of wedlock, a son named Landon Anderson. He would have been in his early twenties when Martin Roker died."

"And in his early forties now," Bradley said, the puzzle pieces fitting together. Landon Anderson was no doubt Martin Roker's son.

"Roker has only one child on record with his estranged wife, a daughter, Ashley. The son with Wanda Anderson slipped through the cracks in the databases."

"I can't thank you enough for going the

extra mile on this," Bradley said. "And thank Eden for me if you talk to her before I do."

"I will," Mitch said. "And no problem. Your dad and I went way back. He mentored me when I worked on the force years ago. He's the reason I went into this work. He was always looking ahead, thinking about the next thing on the horizon, as far as forensic evidence."

"He was a great guy and a fantastic police officer. I was very fortunate that he took me and my sister in."

"Funny you say that. He always used to tell me how blessed he was to have a son and a daughter he could be so proud of. Take care, Bradley. Call me anytime."

He disconnected, and Bradley dropped the phone on the desk, booting up his computer and logging in to the police database remotely. He input the names and birth dates, waiting as the system processed his request.

"Everything okay?" Penny called through the closed door.

"Yeah. Come on in," he responded as he scanned the information he'd pulled up.

She opened the door, yawning and stretching. "What are you doing?"

"I think I may know who's been stalking Sasha Eastman," he responded.

"Who?" she asked, walking across the room and leaning over his shoulder.

He tapped the photo on the screen. "Landon Anderson." He read the name on the man's driver's license. "Martin Roker's look-alike son."

"But why?" Penny asked, dropping onto the bed the way she had so many times in the past.

He would miss that when she was gone.

He would miss having late-night conversations with a sister who was more like a daughter to him.

"I don't know, but I plan to find out and stop him."

"Hopefully sooner rather than later. Being stalked by Gage was a horrible experience. I still have nightmares about it."

"Is that why you're awake?"

"I'm awake because I heard you come in, and I wanted to check in with you. Make sure things were going okay." There was something she wasn't saying. He could hear it in her voice.

"What's wrong, Penny?" he asked.

"Nothing."

"Something," he corrected, and she smiled.

"I just… Things are changing, you know? I'm going to get married and move away, and you're going to be here alone."

"King is offended by that statement," he joked, hoping to lighten her mood.

"King understands what I'm saying. He doesn't want you to be lonely, either."

"I'm not going to be lonely, and you don't need to worry about me."

"We've always been a team, Bradley."

"We still will be. You'll just have a slightly more important member added to your part of our little group."

"Slightly?" She laughed, standing up and swatting him on the shoulder. "How about differently important?"

"Fine. We'll call it that," he replied, looking into her face and seeing her as she was. An adult. Accomplished and hardworking. Smart. Loyal. She was nothing like their biological parents and everything that he had ever hoped for her.

"Why are you looking at me like that?" she said, grabbing his hand and pulling him to his feet.

"Because I'm proud of you and happy for you, and I don't want you to waste another second worrying about what's going to happen to me when you're gone."

"That's like me telling you not to worry. Say it all you want, but I'm still going to be concerned. I love you, Bradley. You are the best big brother a girl could have."

"I love you, too. That won't ever change. Now go back to bed! You have to work in the morning."

She gave him a quick hug and walked out of the room, closing the door behind her. The little girl he would have done almost anything to protect now a grown woman in love, getting married, planning her future.

He prayed she would be happy. That her life would be all the things it hadn't been when their biological parents were raising them.

And he prayed that she would never know the truth: that the house was going to feel a whole lot emptier without her in it.

NINE

The phone rang at just after five in the morning.

Sasha was wide-awake, doing her best to focus on the script she was writing for Wednesday's show. She'd had a restless night, filled with nightmares. In all of them, Martin Roker was chasing her through the streets of Brooklyn, screaming that she was next.

She shuddered, pushing the thought from her mind as she grabbed the phone. "Hello?"

"It's Bradley. Sorry for calling so early, but we've had a break in the case, and I wanted to keep you updated."

"What kind of break?" She sat up straight,

her pulse racing with a mixture of excitement and dread.

"We got a DNA hit from an ancestry database, and we traced the sample to Roker's forty-one-year-old son, Landon."

"He had a son?" she asked, shocked by
the news. She'd thought he had only had
a daughter with his estranged wife, the
woman he'd left to pursue Sasha's mother.

"Landon Anderson. The result of an
affair Martin had with a woman named
Wanda Anderson. She'd filed a restraining
order against him. According to records,
Landon was a computer tech for a public
school on Staten Island until recently."

"Like his father." That was how Martin
and Sasha's mother had met—in the computer lab at the school where she taught.

"Right. From what I've been able to
gather, he had a few other of his father's…
characteristics."

"Like?"

"He became obsessed with a teacher at
the school. She filed a protective order,

and he lost his job. After that, he moved to Brooklyn."

"Why?"

"That's a good question. I'm hoping to ask him. We have a search warrant for his residence and are outside his apartment complex. I've got to go, but I wanted you to be in the loop."

"Be careful," she managed to say before he could end the call.

"I will be," he responded, his voice so soft and warm, she was smiling when she set the phone down.

She expected he would call back within the hour.

She'd worked the crime beat for enough years to know how quickly the police moved in on suspects. She'd interviewed witnesses and knew that a person could be in bed one minute and in a police car the next.

She tried to concentrate on the script.

When that didn't work, she turned on the television, flipping through news channels, hoping to find a story about Landon

Anderson being led from his apartment in handcuffs.

Nothing there.

She tried the internet, googling the name.

Tried the police beat.

If they'd found him, they weren't making it public.

She glanced at her watch, talked herself out of calling Bradley. He'd said he would contact her with updates. She didn't want to interrupt whatever he was doing. Especially if what he was doing was dangerous.

But she was on edge and filled with nervous energy.

If she hadn't promised that she would stay in the room, she would have jogged up and down the hotel stairs a few times, just to get rid of some of her restlessness.

She made the bed, opened the curtains and tried her best not to think about what Bradley and his team were doing. She wanted Landon Anderson caught. She didn't want anyone hurt in the process.

Knowing that a police officer or his K-9 partner had been injured or killed pursuing the son of the man who had killed her mother would only compound the heartbreak.

She shut down her computer, too preoccupied to try to work.

When her phone rang, she answered quickly, not even looking at the caller ID. "Bradley?"

"No, sorry. It's Prudence."

"What's up?" she asked, crossing the room impatiently and staring out the window. There was nothing to see. She was twenty stories up, overlooking the busy street.

"How are you feeling? You went through quite a scare yesterday."

"I'm good. A little sore, but nothing that a few aspirin won't cure."

"Camera ready for Monday? If not, we can run next weekend's programming early."

"A couple bruises. They should be easy to hide with makeup." She glanced at the mirror, hoping that was the case. She hadn't paid much attention when she'd taken her shower. She hadn't bothered drying her hair, not planning to go to the office until Bradley could bring her there.

She had learned her lesson the previous day about leaving the safety of a locked room. She planned to stay where she was until Bradley told her Landon had been arrested.

"I'm glad to hear it, Sasha. You know how much I care about you, and I hate to put pressure on you, but I've told some higher-ups that we're going to run your story next week, and they're planning to do a preview Monday. I won't be in the office from noon today until early Monday morning. They're planning on stopping by at nine. I really need you to come through for me on this."

"You know I will, Prudence," she promised, her stomach churning with anxiety.

She enjoyed her job.

She didn't want to lose it because Martin Roker's son had decided to stalk her.

"Then you'll be here by eleven? That'll give us plenty of time to review the tape and discuss the changes I'd like you to make. I hate to ask you to work tomorrow—"

"I'll get everything done. You have my promise," Sasha assured her, glancing at her watch and frowning. It was closing in on nine. With traffic, it would take at least thirty minutes to get to the office. She could leave as late as ten and still make it in time, but she didn't dare leave later than that.

She brushed her hair, pulled it into a loose bun, swept on a coat of mascara and slid into slacks and a turtleneck. She layered with a bright yellow cardigan and slid her feet into ankle boots. No heels. Just a dab of concealer over the bruises on her cheek. A coat of clear gloss, and she was ready to go.

She paced the hotel room until ten, glancing at her watch so often she grew impatient with herself. Either things hadn't gone as Bradley had hoped, or he was busy at the station, questioning Landon or booking him into the detention center.

Either way, she was between a rock and a hard place.

If she left the hotel room, she'd be breaking her promise to him. If she didn't, she be breaking the one she had made to Prudence. She had no desire to do either, but she knew Bradley and the K-9 team were searching for Landon. For all she knew, he'd left the city and was deep in hiding. He'd be a fool to keep coming after her now the police knew who he was, and she had no doubt he was aware of what they'd discovered. By this time, they'd been to his apartment, searched it, had probably put out an APB on him and any vehicle that might be registered in his name.

His minutes of freedom were numbered.

And if she wasn't careful, her days with a job would be, too. Prudence had always been fair and reasonable, but people who didn't do their jobs, and do them well, didn't last long. She had no problem praising news anchors who did good work, and she had no problem firing ones who did not.

For the past three years, Sasha had stayed in the former category. She couldn't afford to slip into the latter one. Her father hadn't had life insurance. His life savings had been eaten up by medical expenses. By the time he'd passed away, he'd been broke, and she had been paying co-pays and deductibles for his treatment. Her finances had been stretched thin, her savings accounts emptied.

Two years later, and she was finally out of the hole, building a nest egg and standing on secure financial footing. Losing her job would ruin that, and it was a chance she didn't dare take.

She checked her watch one last time, searching her phone screen as if a call might have come through unnoticed.

She knew it hadn't, and she left the room with her purse hiked over her shoulder, a wool peacoat thrown across her arm. If she needed to stay at the hotel for another few days, she'd have to return home to grab more clothes. She'd worry about that after her meeting with Prudence was over.

She waited in the hotel lobby while a concierge called a taxi service for her, then sat in the back, fidgeting with her phone as they made their way to the office. She didn't want to interrupt Bradley's day, but she didn't want to go to the office without letting him know she'd be there. If he went to the hotel, and she wasn't there, he'd be worried.

On the other hand, he might be in a dangerous situation.

A phone call might distract him.

If he was meeting with his sergeant, he might not appreciate his phone ringing.

She listed pros and cons, worrying over the decision like a teenage girl trying to decide if she should contact her first crush. That thought, more than any other, helped her decide. She was a grown woman. She needed to act like one. She needed to contact Bradley. He had given her his number. There was absolutely no logical reason not to give him a call.

She dialed his number quickly as the taxi approached her building. The phone rang once and then went to voice mail. She left a brief message, letting him know what had happened and that she would be at the office for the rest of the day.

She dropped the phone into her bag as she exited the taxi and hurried into the building. There were several people chatting in the lobby, their dark suits and polished shoes making her think they were part of the financial adviser group that owned an office suite down the hall from the studio.

She was glad that she wasn't alone, that the building had people moving around and conducting business. She didn't think Landon would dare come to the office building again, but from what Bradley had said, he wasn't in his right mind. It was difficult to predict what he would do.

She took the stairs two at a time, hurrying down the hall and through the cable network's doors. As it was most days, the receptionist desk was empty, the computer screen dark. The light next to the door behind it glowed green, indicating that there was no one in the broadcasting studio.

That wasn't a surprise. On the weekend, most programming was recorded, and the station ran on a bare-bones crew. She hung her coat on the hook and headed to her office. She'd arrived in time to review the work she had done the previous day. She had been too emotional to judge her work then. Today, she should be able to see it through clearer eyes.

She had locked her office door when she'd left for the day, and she pulled out her key. But the door was open. She stepped back, her heart slamming against her ribs as she peered through the doorway.

Everything looked the way she'd left it. Laptop closed, chair pushed in. Phone on the corner of the desk. Coffee pot washed and sitting upside down on a pile of paper towel.

"Maybe you didn't lock it after all," she

murmured as she stepped into the office and closed the door.

"Of course you did," a man said as the cold butt of a gun jabbed into her side.

She froze in terror, every thought flying from her head as she met the cold dead eyes of Martin Roker's son.

"Don't scream," he said. "Don't try to run. I can kill you where you're standing and sleep like a baby tonight."

"What do you want, Landon?" she asked, hoping that using his name would throw him off-balance and make him lower his guard.

"Justice for my father," he responded, his eyes a clear gray-blue that was as cold and hard as a frozen lake.

"What do you mean?"

"Don't pretend you don't know. That will just make me angry." He shoved the gun deeper into her side.

"I'm not pretending. I really don't know. I was only fourteen when my mother was killed."

"Your mother," he nearly spit, "was an

adulterer. My father was going to marry my mother until he met your mother. Her sin cost my father his life."

"Your father had a wife and daughter," she pointed out. "He cheated on his wife with your mother."

Rage flashed in Landon's eyes. "No. My dad would have married my mom. He was leaving his wife to be with my mother, Wanda Anderson. That's why I hold no grudge against his wife or daughter, my half sister. But then he met your mother."

Sasha had no idea of the timeline of all this—whom Martin had met first. Bradley had said Landon's mother had filed a restraining order against Martin, so clearly she wasn't trying to get back together with the man. Likely, she wanted to keep herself and her son away from Martin Roker.

Sasha was filled with regret over her mother's choice to get involved with Martin and would never understand it. But that wasn't the point here. Landon Anderson was clearly delusional and had shifted the blame for what happened or didn't happen in his own family to Sasha's mother. And now to Sasha herself.

"My parents would have been happily married if it weren't for your mother!" he growled at her.

"You're delusional," she said, the words slipping out before she could stop them.

"Grief will do that to a person."

"I've been grieving my mother for eighteen years. It hasn't driven me mad yet."

"Because you're as coldhearted as your mother. You don't care about anyone but yourself." He jabbed her again, pushing her to the door. "We're going to walk out of here, take the elevator down to the lobby and go out the rear entrance of the building. My car is just outside the door. If you scream, if you call for help, if you do anything to try to escape, I will shoot you and anyone who happens to be nearby."

"I'll cooperate," she said, unwilling to risk other people's lives for the sake of her own. Maybe when they stepped outside, she could fight for her freedom. For now, she had no choice but to walk out of the room and lead the way to the elevators. She hoped that Prudence would appear, or that a security guard would notice how tense and scared she looked and ask if everything was okay, but they made it out of the office and into the elevator without drawing the attention of anyone.

She was relieved.

She was also terrified.

Once they left the building and she got into Landon's car, there was every chance she'd disappear. Never to be seen again. There. Gone. Vanished without a trace. There would be news stories about her, speculation about where she had gone and whom she had been with. Anniversary vigils where people prayed for her safe return.

If Landon had his way, she never would.

She understood that.

She just wasn't sure how to stop him without hurting anyone else.

"Move," he demanded as the elevator doors slid open.

She did as he said, stumbling off the elevator, her body nearly numb with fear. The group of people who had been in the lobby were gone, and her boots echoed hollow against the tile floor as she walked toward the back entrance.

When her phone rang, she let out a quiet shriek.

"Shut up or I'll make you sorry you didn't," Landon hissed.

"I need to answer my phone," she responded, her voice shaking with fear.

"No."

"It's the police detective who helped me yesterday. We were supposed to meet here at eleven," she lied, knowing that the time would worry him. "He's probably calling to confirm."

"Answer it. Tell him you can't meet."

"He'll ask why, and then—"

"I said answer it," he growled.

She pretended to do so reluctantly, her head down to hide the relief in her eyes. "Hello?"

"Sasha? Bradley. Sorry it took me so

long to get back to you. We were tied up at Landon's apartment."

"No problem, Detective McGregor," she responded, pressing the phone tightly to her ear and hoping Landon couldn't hear Bradley's end of the conversation.

"Everything okay?" Bradley asked, obviously noticing her use of his title and last name.

"No," she replied. "Not at all. Work is hectic. I won't be able to meet you at my office."

Please let him realize I'm in trouble. Please, God.

"Work?" he repeated.

"The project? It's more complicated than I thought, and I'm going to need more time to prep for it. If you don't mind, I'd rather meet with you tomorrow."

"That's fine," he said, a sharp edge to his voice.

He'd caught on. She could hear the concern mixed with cold determination.

"You're at the office now?" he asked.

"Stepping out for an early lunch."

"I see. Any idea where you're going?"

"Finish the conversation and hang up!" Landon whispered, pushing the gun into her ribs with so much force she knew she'd have a bruise.

If help didn't come quickly, that would be the least of her worries.

"Listen, I've got to go. How about you call me later?" she said.

"Is he there?" Bradley asked.

"Yes. I'll do that. Thank you," she responded, pretending to end the call and dropping the phone back into her purse.

"Leave it here," Landon demanded.

"But—"

"Drop it. On the floor. Now." His face was red with rage, his eyes blazing.

She pulled it out of her bag and dropped it, hoping the line had stayed open. "Where are we going?" she asked.

"One of my father's favorite spots," he responded.

"Your father was a computer guy. A computer store? A technology museum?" She didn't move as he had told her to, just stood near the phone, hoping the conversation was getting through to Bradley.

"That's how much you know. He loved the ocean. He used to spend his days off at Manhattan Beach Park. He always thought it was odd that there was a neighborhood in Brooklyn named after a different borough."

"Manhattan Beach Park?" she repeated loudly. "There are a lot of people there this time of day."

"Not this time of year, and not when the sun goes down. I'm willing to wait for that," he responded, shoving her forward. "Now move!"

She had no choice but to obey, so she took one slow step after another toward the exit, praying all the while that Bradley had heard every word she'd said.

Bradley and King waited on the east side of a rocky outcropping that jutted out into the ocean. Cold air seeped through Bradley's jacket, salty spray coating his hair and skin. He'd been in place for fifteen minutes, his body tense as he waited for the call he was hoping to hear: Roker's son had arrived, and he had Sasha with him.

If he had heard right, if Landon was telling the truth, this was where they'd headed after they'd left Sasha's office. Landon's apartment complex was just a few blocks away. No water view, but a nice enough property for someone who didn't seem to have a way of supporting himself. They'd just finished collecting evidence when Bradley had called Sasha. He had planned to give her an update and let her know he was on his way to the hotel. Instead, he had interrupted her kidnapping.

His blood ran cold at the thought, and he prayed that he wasn't mistaken, and that Sasha and Landon were on the way to Manhattan Beach Park. His sergeant and Henry were waiting with their K-9s near the entrance of the park, hidden from view. They'd radio and trail Landon when he arrived.

Bradley was on the beach, ready to release King as soon as the perp was in sight. They'd cleared the area, stationing plainclothes police officers at entrances to the beach and to various areas of the park, but Bradley thought Landon would come here. The sound of waves would mute a gunshot, and a body could easily be tossed into the ocean and carried out with the tide.

If that was the plan, it wasn't flawless. As a matter of fact, it seemed more an act of desperation than a planned effort. Either way, the results would be the same, if the team didn't stop him.

He shivered. And not from the cold wind carrying off the Atlantic.

His radio crackled, and the sergeant's voice carried over the sound of crashing waves. "We've spotted them leaving a black Honda Accord. Heading toward the beach. I'm following."

"Copy," Bradley said, staying where he was, stomach to the ground, gaze focused through a crack between boulders.

He needed to bide his time and wait things out. If he showed his hand too soon, Sasha could be injured.

As he watched, two figures appeared, walking from the area of the beach closest to the parking lot. A tall, stooped man, his arm around a slim woman.

"I've got them," he murmured into the radio, never taking his eyes off the approaching figures.

"Copy," the sergeant replied. "We're a hundred yards behind. There's a clear path, if you want to release King."

"They're too far away. If I let him go now, Landon might have a chance to shoot him or Sasha."

"Copy. We're hanging back. Don't wait too long, McGregor. This guy has already proved he's a loose cannon."

He was right.

There was no question about that, but Bradley resisted the urge to give in to fear. Sasha and Landon were in full view of several beachfront restaurants. There were patrons inside, looking out the windows and taking in the views. Men like Landon Anderson worked under the cover of darkness or in the shadowy corners of the world where most people never went. If he'd had to guess, Bradley would say the perp planned to cross the small sandy beach and lead Sasha into a less-visible area of the park.

They weren't going to get that far.

He waited, counting the seconds as the figures drew closer. He could see Sasha's pale face, her wind-whipped cheeks and sand-speckled slacks. He could also see the gun pressed to her side. One wrong move and a shot would be fired straight into her abdomen.

He tensed, and King shifted restlessly. The Malinois could sense his anxiety and was reacting to it.

"Wait," he murmured, knowing the dog wouldn't move until given the command.

Sasha stumbled, and she fell to her hands and knees, her hair falling out of the loose bun and hanging around her face.

"Get up!" Landon bellowed, the words carried clearly on the ocean breeze. "Now!"

She pushed to her feet, her hands fisted, the wind blowing her hair toward Landon. She lifted her hands, opening both so that sand flew straight into his face. He fell back, clawing at his eyes. She sprinted toward the outcrop, probably hoping to use it as a shield.

"NYPD! Down on the ground or I'll release my dog," Bradley shouted, hoping Sasha heard and praying she would obey.

She dropped to the ground.

Landon took off, racing back the way he'd come, perhaps thinking, mistakenly, that he could outrun a dog.

"I said, down on the ground!" Bradley repeated.

Landon kept going, obviously knowing that if he fired his weapon, he'd be shot before he could take his next breath.

"Get him!" Bradley urged.

King sprang over the walls, bounding across the sand in a blur of tan fur and unbridled energy.

TEN

It happened fast

One minute, Landon was running back toward the parking lot.

The next he was on the ground, the wrist of his gun hand between King's razor-sharp teeth.

"Call him off!" Landon screamed. "Call him off."

"In a minute," Bradley said as he walked past Sasha, knelt next to Landon and lifted the gun he had dropped, emptying the cartridge.

"Release," he commanded, and King backed away, still growling ferociously and showing his teeth.

If Sasha had been Landon, she wouldn't have dared move.

Landon didn't seem to have the same compunctions. He started to push to his knees, and King lunged for him again.

"I wouldn't do that if I were you," Bradley said dispassionately. "My dog doesn't like it."

"You've got no right to do this. I've done nothing wrong," Landon bellowed.

"Nothing? How about kidnapping and attempted murder?"

"Prove I wasn't just out here having a lover's spat with my girlfriend."

Sasha snorted, the dampness of the sand seeping through her slacks, the salty water making the cut on her chin sting. She didn't dare move, though. Not with King standing guard a few feet away.

She waited while Bradley frisked and cuffed Landon.

When he finished, he turned in her direction. "Are you okay?" he asked, offering a hand and pulling her to her feet.

"Fine. Just glad you and King showed up when you did. I don't think Landon was planning to let me walk off this beach alive."

"You're as mouthy and obnoxious as your mother was. You know that?" Landon said, his cold blue eyes staring into hers.

"You didn't know her," Bradley said. "You were living on Staten Island with your mom until you moved a year ago."

"You've been doing your research, haven't you, Detective?"

"It's my job. And called your mother, too. She filled me in on some details."

Landon scowled. "She needs to keep her mouth shut."

"Not when she's being questioned by the police, and not when she could go to jail if she refuses to cooperate," Bradley responded, calling information into his radio and then reading Landon his Miranda rights.

Minutes later, two familiar K-9 officers appeared, striding across the beach and hauling Landon to his feet. She'd seen both of them outside her office when Bradley had called in the bomb threat and again at the K-9 unit the previous day. The taller man was Detective Henry Roarke, who had a beagle named Cody. The other was Bradley's boss, Sergeant Gavin Sutherland, whose K-9 partner was a springer spaniel named Tommy. He'd assured her that they were doing everything that they could to find the person who had attacked her.

Now it was over, Landon Anderson in handcuffs and defeated, his eyes flashing with impotent rage.

"Are you all right, Ms. Eastman?" Sergeant Sutherland asked.

"Fine."

"You're sure? We can call you an ambulance, if you need one."

"I'm sure."

"You're going to pay for this one day," Landon cut in, shooting venom in her direction.

"I haven't done anything," she responded.

"Your mother killed my father."

"The police killed your father," Bradley corrected.

"No, his love and passion for a woman who used him and threw him away were what put him in the crosshairs of the police," Landon snapped. "If not for her mother, he would still be alive."

"And you think killing her daughter will bring your father back to life?" Detective Roarke asked.

"No, but it will make me feel like justice has finally prevailed."

Sasha knew Landon had everything twisted in his mind. The anniversary of her mother's murder was also the anniversary of his father's death, which had clearly triggered his rage, his need for revenge. There would not have been a marriage or getting back together or a family unit for the three of them. His mother had moved to Staten Island to get away from Martin Roker.

Now his look-alike son couldn't hurt Sasha anymore. It was over.

"You can explain all that to your lawyer, Anderson," Sergeant Sutherland said with a tired sigh. "Come on. Let's get you booked. We'll see you back at the station, Bradley."

He and Detective Roarke led Landon away.

Sasha watched them go, her legs weak in the aftermath of what had happened.

She'd been kidnapped again.

Nearly killed again.

"How about you sit for a minute?" Bradley suggested, his arm suddenly around her waist, his fingers curved around her bottom ribs.

She wanted to tell him she was fine, but that wasn't true.

She was far from it.

She dropped onto one of the nearby boulders, her hands shaking as she pulled her hair back into a bun.

"That was a clever trick," Bradley said as he took a seat beside her.

"What?"

"Sand in the eyes."

"I wasn't sure what else to do. I didn't

know you and other members of the K-9 team were around, and I knew he planned to kill me if he got me far enough from prying eyes." She shuddered, and he dropped an arm around her shoulders, pulling her close to his side. He was solid, muscular and warm, and it felt right to lean her head against his shoulder.

"You were supposed to stay in the hotel room," he reminded her gently.

"Prudence insisted I come to the office. I left you a message, so you'd know where I was. I figured you guys were handling Landon, and I'd be safe. It was a stupid assumption."

"Not stupid, but it could have cost you your life."

"I know. I'm sorry."

"No need to apologize. You're safe. The perp is going to be put away."

"All's well that ends well?"

"Exactly. And this has ended particularly well for King. We're in one of his favorite places. Mind if I let him chase a few gulls before I bring you back to the hotel?"

"That was the plan for the afternoon," she reminded him.

He smiled, brushing a strand of hair from her cheek, his finger warm against her cold skin. "You're right. It was. Not quite the way I imagined everything going down, but King won't care."

At the mention of his name, the dog's ears perked up, and his tongue lolled out.

"All right, buddy. Go do your thing," Bradley said, waving his hand toward birds that were swooping low over the water.

King leaped forward, springing across the sand with unbridled enthusiasm. Sasha stayed where she was, Bradley's arm still around her shoulders. He was a comforting solid presence, and she knew if she allowed herself, she could get used to having him around.

When Bradley's phone rang, she almost told him to ignore it.

She wanted to stay where she was, basking in the warmth of the sun and cool dampness of the ocean breeze as she watched King chase seagulls along the shore.

He pulled it from his pocket and frowned as he glanced at the number.

"Is everything okay?" she asked, all the peacefulness of the day slipping away.

"It looks like someone from your work is calling," he said as he answered. "Hello? Yes, it is. She's with me. She ran into some trouble, but she's fine now. All right. Sure. I'll give her your message."

"Was it Prudence?" she asked, jumping up and brushing sand from her pants. "I forgot. I'm supposed to be meeting with her." She patted her pockets, trying to find her cell phone.

"If you're looking for your cell phone, the security guard found it and brought it to your office. When Prudence realized you'd been there and were missing, she got worried and decided to call me. She asked mc to tell you that she has to leave for her appointment, but she trusts you to have a great presentation for Monday. She'll see you then."

"That's not what she was saying an hour ago," she muttered.

"But it's what she's saying now, so how about I take you back to the hotel, you get your things and I bring you home? I'm sure you're ready to get back to your normal routine."

"I'm ready, but I'd rather get my things, go to the K-9 unit to make my statement and then go home. I can take a taxi if that's going to be any trouble for you."

"We're past the point of you worrying about that."

"What?"

"You being any trouble to me."

"How do you figure that?" she asked, laughing as King rushed over and shook water from his sleek coat.

"When you go through near-death experiences together, you become friends. Friends are never a bother to one another."

She laughed again. "Near death? I don't think it was that desperate of a situation."

"Landon would have shot both of us, if he'd had the opportunity," he said.

"Probably," she agreed.

"That's about as near death as I want to be today. Of course, if you'd rather back out of the friendship thing, I'll understand." He smiled, and her heart did a funny little flip.

"Back out? Just when I realized what one of the perks is?" she said, her gaze tracking King as he bounded back to the shoreline. "I don't think so."

"Perks?"

"Afternoons at the beach with a really handsome dog and a really nice guy."

His smile broadened. "In that case, how about we get out of here? Once we finish at the K-9 unit, I'll treat you to dinner."

"Another perk?"

"Something like that." He offered his hand, and she took it, her fingers threading through his as he called for King to heel and started walking back to the parking lot.

And it felt so right to be walking hand

in hand with him, to have King loping along beside them. It didn't feel strained or scary or uncertain. It felt comfortable and sweet. It felt like belonging.

She wasn't sure how she felt about that.

But she knew when this was over, when her statement had been given and she said goodbye to Bradley and King knowing that the danger was over and they could all go back to the lives they had lived before Landon appeared, her life would feel just a little emptier than it had before.

Getting Sasha's statement and writing up his report had taken longer than Bradley anticipated. Not because the tasks were more arduous than usual. Because the team had been eager to hear the details of Landon's apprehension. Sasha had waited with good humor and patience while Bradley, Gavin and Henry filled everyone in.

Then she waited longer while he typed up his report.

She petted King and played with Cody,

the adorable beagle, then poured two cups
of coffee from the carafe and handed one
to him. If she were bothered by the long
wait, she wasn't letting on. If anything,
she seemed to be enjoying her time with
the dogs.

And, he had to admit, he enjoyed his
time with her.

Even at the precinct, having her around
made him feel more content than he had
in a long time. He didn't want to read too
much into that. He certainly didn't want
to create something out of nothing.

But what he was beginning to feel for
Sasha wasn't nothing. It was new, interesting, intriguing. Unexpected.

And now that Landon had been apprehended, she was safe. Free to go back
to her life while he went back to his. He
shouldn't feel disappointed about that, but
he did.

"Thanks," he said, taking a quick sip
before setting the mug down. He didn't
meet her eyes. He didn't want her to see
the softness in his gaze, the warmth he felt

toward her. He didn't want to make her uncomfortable or make himself seem to be overstepping boundaries. "I'm almost finished here."

"There's no rush," she replied with a smile. "I'm sure if I get bored sitting here, I can find more dogs to play with."

"Easily. Everyone on the K-9 team has a partner. And we also have a mama dog named Brooke and her puppies. She was a stray."

"The one with five puppies? I read a story about that in the news. You guys spent a couple weeks trying to locate her puppies, right?"

"Right, and once we found them, someone came forward and claimed them as his."

"Then why do you still have them?"

"When one of our officers went to deliver her to the owner, he found a backyard breeder and a lot of sick German shepherd dogs. We closed it down and arrested the guy."

"And the dogs?"

"They got the vet care they needed, and they went to good homes. Brooke and her puppies are staying with the K-9 unit. Brooke is currently training to be in the program."

"Really?" she asked, glancing around as if she expected to see them romping through the precinct. "Are they here today? I'd love to meet them."

"I can introduce you one day," he said, watching her as she reached down to pet King again. "You know, it's funny."

"What?"

"When we met, you didn't seem much of a dog person."

"When we met, I'd never been around a dog like King," she replied.

"He is quite the dog," Bradley agreed as he finally typed the last sentence of the report and saved the document. "You ready to go back to your apartment? Maybe you need some rest after what you've been through. I can take you to dinner after that."

She smiled. "I'm not tired. As a matter

of fact, I've been thinking a story about your K-9 unit might be in the future. Unless you think that's not a good idea?"

"It'll be a better idea after we solve the Emery murders," he said as he powered down his computer and stood.

"Why do you say that?" she asked.

"The public isn't pleased with how long it's taking."

"Maybe because they don't understand everything else your team does," she suggested. "A clear look at how the team operates, how the dogs are trained and all the time and energy that the K-9 unit expends making certain the city is safe might open people's eyes."

"You might have a point, but we're swamped right now and pretty focused on our goals." He didn't want to discourage her. He thought the story sounded like a good idea, but now really wasn't the time. Until they found the person who had murdered the Emerys, every spare minute the unit had was being poured into solving the case.

"Is that a kind way of saying you don't want me to do it, Bradley?" she asked as they walked outside.

"Not at all. I'm just saying now might not be the best time."

"Because of the Emery case."

"Right." He fished keys out of his pocket and walked to his Jeep, opening the passenger door so Sasha could slide in. He opened the hatch so King could hop in his crate, then slid in behind the wheel.

"Can I ask you something?" Sasha said.

"Sure."

"Is the Emery case more important because of its similarities to your parents'?"

He wanted to tell her it wasn't.

That was the correct answer.

It was the one an objective law enforcement officer would be able to give.

He wasn't objective. Not when it came to this.

"Off the record," she added. "Of course."

"Why do you ask?"

"Answering a question with a question

is a great way of shifting the focus of a conversation."

"Maybe it is, and maybe that's what I'm trying to do," he admitted. "I can tell you honestly that the team hasn't put any more time into the Emery case than we would any other investigation."

"But?"

"I'd be lying if I said the investigation hasn't hit close to home on two levels. First, one of our own fell in love with Lucy Emery's aunt, remember? Detective Nate Slater was the first responder to the Emery house, and he and Willow are now raising Lucy. Finding the killer is personal for the Brooklyn K-9 Unit on that end. And for me, yeah, the case has stirred up old memories. The killer chose the twentieth anniversary of my parents' murders to strike. Wore a similar clown mask with blue hair, gave Lucy a stuffed monkey." He shook his head and ran a hand through his hair. "How can the killer still be on the loose?"

"You'll get him," she said, having no

doubt he and his dedicated, hardworking colleagues would do just that. "Just like you got your parents' murderer."

He nodded. "That was an unexpected bonus. After twenty years, I'd almost given up hope that would happen. The copycat case led to the retesting of old evidence from my parents' crime scene— a watchband. We'd been hoping to find a DNA connection between the two cases and didn't, but at least retesting resulted in a match from a genealogy site and right to Randall Gage."

"I can't imagine having to wait that long for justice."

"Then you'll understand why this particular case is so important to me. I don't want Lucy Emery to have to wait. Not like Penelope and I did. I want her to have her answers, so she can move forward with her life and not be chained to the past by a bunch of unknowns."

"I do understand that," she said. "Maybe I shouldn't have asked such a personal question."

"I don't mind. If I hadn't wanted to answer, I wouldn't have," he replied, surprising himself with the comment. Even more surprised that he meant it. He didn't like sharing pieces of himself. In the past, people's questions had felt intrusive and accusatory, unwelcome and unnecessary. But Sasha was different. She had a sincerity about her, a genuine curiosity and desire to understand that he both respected and admired. It was her warmth, though, that made him willing to open up to her, the fact that she had lived through her own heartache and that she so carefully approached the pain and heartache of others. There seemed to be no voyeurism, no desire to do anything other than understand. And there was a small part of him that wanted her to know the way he thought, the things that had shaped him, the way the past had made him the man he was.

"I'm glad you did share," she responded. "Since I did, maybe you will."

"Will what?"

"Share."

"You won't know unless you ask a question," she said.

"All right, how about this," he began.

"Ask a reasonable one," she added hurriedly, the humor in her eyes making him smile.

"Are you hungry?"

Her eyes widened in surprise, and she laughed. "I'm always hungry."

"Want to sit down or bring something home?" he asked, wanting to reach forward and brush a stray strand of hair from her cheek, feel the softness of her skin. She was a beautiful woman. He had noticed that the first day they'd met, but her spirit—the essence of who she was— made her nearly irresistible.

"What will King do if we eat in?" she asked, her concern for the Malinois only making her more attractive.

"Behave while he waits. Get rewarded when we return."

"I'd rather he not have to wait."

"Then we'll grab something and bring it home. Your place or mine?"

"Mine. Then you won't have to leave home to drop me off after we eat."

"I don't mind."

"I do," she replied.

"Okay. Here's another question for you—burgers, Chinese or Italian?"

"I think King prefers burgers."

"And you?" he pressed, amused and still very touched by her concern for his K-9 partner. This was what he would want if he wanted a relationship—a woman who understood his commitment to the job and his relationship to King, who thought about those things when she planned meals or outings. Someone who was laid-back and accepting, but strong, too. Sasha was all those things.

"Tonight, I prefer burgers, too."

"Burgers it is," he said, pulling out of the parking lot and onto the busy street. The Emery case was still weighing on him, the desire to solve it and provide the closure Lucy would one day need something he woke with every morning and went to bed with every night.

But as he drove to a burger place to order their meals, Bradley felt lighter than he had in years, his focus on more than work, dog training and Penny.

Maybe his future didn't just have to include those things.

Maybe there was room for more.

A life outside his job. Relationships that weren't built in the confines of the headquarters building.

Maybe he could have what his adoptive parents had—the warmth of a family and of home.

It was something he hadn't dared to consider before, but every time he looked into Sasha's eyes, he felt like he was glimpsing a future he had never dared believe he could have.

He glanced her way, realized she'd been watching him, a soft smile playing at the corner of her lips.

"What?" he asked, wondering what she was thinking.

"I like you, Detective," she responded.

"That's it?"

"Does there have to be more?"

"No," he replied, surprised by the simplicity of it, by the easy way they had fallen into each other's lives. His life had never been easy. He had devoted his teenage years and his adulthood to making certain Penny was okay and to proving himself as a police officer. He had gone after justice the way other people chased after dreams. He had never considered himself to be a family man. He certainly hadn't thought of himself as husband material. Relationships were for people who had more time and energy to devote to them. For people who were hardwired for love and who were open to it.

He had spent too many years observing his parents' relationship, too many decades seeing the heartbreaking truth of what could happen in romantic relationships. He had ridden in ambulances and listened to beaten women sob because the person who had hurt them was the person they loved the most.

And he had told himself that he was better off without romance and love, better off keeping his thoughts and energy focused on his job.

He wasn't capable of physically hurting a woman, but he didn't want to be responsible for neglecting the feelings of someone who cared about him. He didn't want to have children waiting at home for him to return after a long weekend spent working homicide cases. He didn't want to hurt anyone with his absorption with his job and with justice.

But he couldn't deny the truth of how he felt about Sasha.

He reached for her hand, squeezing it gently as he pulled up in front of the burger place. "You know what?" he asked.

"What?"

"I like you, too."

She laughed, and he leaned across the console, kissing her gently as King shifted impatiently in his crate and sighed. Maybe the dog knew better than Bradley did just how deeply he would feel the kiss, and how desperately he would long for more.

Not just physical touch, but conversation, communication, laughter. All the things he had told himself he didn't need and shouldn't want.

All the things he suddenly wondered if he could have.

Without hurting anyone.

Without sacrificing his commitment to the job.

If he was willing. If she was.

ELEVEN

Life had a way of going on.

Sasha had learned that after her mother's death.

Then relearned it after her divorce.

Both times, she had thought her heart was broken beyond repair. She had wondered how the world could remain unchanged when her entire life had fallen apart. Somehow, the sky was just as blue, the bird songs just as cheerful. Summer grass remained soft green. Winter snow still tasted like childhood dreams. One day chased after another. Weeks passed just like they always did.

When her father died, she had already learned the lesson well. She'd grieved, but she had accepted that eventually some of the pain would fade, the heartache wouldn't hurt so much, and she would wake up one morning without the sick feeling of sorrow in the pit of her stomach.

At thirty-two, she was old enough to understand that there were life-changing events.

But Bradley's kiss? That one sweet, gentle touch of his lips?

It hadn't just been life-changing. It had thrown the world out of orbit, left her dizzy and unsure of her footing.

She wasn't supposed to fall in love again.

Because she wasn't willing to have her heart broken again.

That was why she hadn't dated since the divorce.

It was why she had turned down invitations to dinner and lunch, refused blind dates, told her coworkers and friends that she was not interested in entering the dating pool again.

She had meant it.

She *had*.

But somehow that slipped her mind every time Bradley called or texted.

In the week since Landon Anderson's arrest, she had done her best to put some distance between them. She had refused an invitation to lunch, using work as an excuse. When he'd invited her to the dog park one evening, she'd said she was still trying to get a recording edited for the weekend's broadcast.

She had been, but there was more to it than that.

She was afraid of crossing a line with him. One she would never be able to step back over again. He had called them friends, but she knew they were moving toward more than that. Every night, he called her after work, and they chatted for an hour, catching each other up on the details of the day.

Every morning, she told herself that she wouldn't answer the phone the next time, that she'd pretend to be asleep, that she would claim fatigue every night until he stopped calling.

She sighed, pulling her hair up into a high ponytail. She'd pulled on yoga pants and a long-sleeved T-shirt. Most Saturdays she worked in the office for a few hours, but she wasn't in the mood. She had spent too many hours bent over a computer screen, splicing together pieces of the show she had recorded.

She had told her story with as much candor as she could, using old family photos to give viewers a glimpse of the kind of home she had grown up in and the kind of people her parents were. Prudence had previewed the finished product Thursday, and she had raved about the sweet authenticity of it.

Hopefully viewers would be just as touched.

Sasha didn't intend to tune in to the show, but she hadn't been able to sleep in. She was too wound up, too nervous. She hadn't ever told her story before. Not the way she had for the show.

She grabbed a down vest from her closet and slid into it. She'd go for a run. That would get her mind off the show and off Bradley.

She left the apartment, jogging along the still-sleepy sidewalk. The sun had barely risen, and Saturday traffic was light, most people enjoying a little extra sleep.

Her phone rang as she rounded the corner of her block.

She answered it, knowing without looking that Bradley was calling.

"Good morning," she said, her heart doing a strange little flip as she pictured him holding the phone to his ear and sipping coffee.

"Good morning. Sounds like you're outside."

"I decided to go for a run."

"You should have told me. I'd have joined you."

"You have the day off?"

"No. I'm working the afternoon shift. Want to join King and me at the dog park in an hour?" he asked.

She hesitated.

He noticed.

Of course.

"I'm getting the impression that you're not comfortable going out with me."

"I'm comfortable. Too comfortable. That's the problem," she admitted.

"Why is too much comfort a problem?"

"You know I was married before?" She had mentioned it during one of their long conversations.

"Yes."

"And that he left me for someone else?"

"Yes again."

"So maybe you can understand why I'm...nervous about getting into another relationship."

"Nervous? Or unwilling?"

"Just...nervous."

For a moment, he was silent. When he spoke, she could hear disappointment mixed with understanding in his voice. "All right."

"All right?"

"I'm not going to push you, Sasha. When you're ready, I'll be here."

"Bradley, it isn't that I don't want to be

friends—" she began, wanting to stop the conversation before it went too far.

"*I* don't want to be friends," he said firmly. "Not *just* friends, anyway. I want more than that. It would be unfair for both of us to keep moving forward like we are—one of us wanting one thing, the other one something else."

"It's not—"

"Hold on," he said. She could hear a muffled conversation, and then he was back. "Sorry about that. I got called in to work for a meeting. We are about to begin. We plan to discuss our next steps in the Emery case."

"You still haven't located Andy?"

"No, and since that's the only lead we haven't been able to follow up on, we need to. I'm going to have to go. We can discuss things later."

"Bradley," she began, wanting to apologize and tell him that she knew she was being foolish, that in the deepest part of her heart, she wanted exactly what he did.

"I'll call you tonight," he said, and then he was gone.

She dropped the phone into the inside pocket of her vest, then zipped it. The morning was crisp with the first hints of winter, dead leaves skittering across the sidewalk as she continued jogging.

Sheepshead Bay was waking, people rushing along the sidewalk on their way to work or to breakfast. Like Sasha, some people were jogging, dodging through the burgeoning crowd like Alpine skiers dodging slalom poles.

She turned off Ocean Avenue, taking a quieter route on a less-traveled street. She didn't realize where she was heading until she saw the limestone facade of the K-9 unit headquarters.

"Oh no you don't," she muttered, turning off on a side street before she reached it. The last thing she wanted was for one of Bradley's coworkers to see her wandering around outside the building.

She'd talk to him later.

Just like he'd suggested.

When she did, she would try to explain things a little more clearly. Hopefully he would understand.

She turned another corner, jogging into an area of Bay Ridge that wasn't nearly as well kept. Houses were close together, the yards cluttered and overgrown. Several properties were boarded up. There was a day care just ahead. A few blocks down and to the left was the house where Lucy Emery had lived with her parents.

Sasha had spent time in this area when she worked the crime beat, talking to men and women who lived in the area. She slowed down as she passed the day care, smiling at a few parents who were dropping their children off early. Several smiled back, but she didn't want to interrupt their morning routine. Trying to get information from someone heading into work seldom produced results.

She continued down the street, waving at a few older men who sat on rickety porch furniture, smoking cigarettes. "Good morning!" she called.

"You're that lady doing the good-news stories, right?" one of the men said, offering a nearly toothless grin.

"That's right."

"You gonna do a story about this neighborhood?"

"That's why I'm here," she said. "To find out what stories there are to tell."

"Good. Good," the man said, leaving his buddies and crossing his overgrown front yard. An old wrought iron fence surrounded the patch of dead grass. He leaned against the gate and nodded sagely. "Too much bad news coming out of this place lately. Time to change that."

"Bad news? You mean like the murder that happened a few months ago?" she asked.

"I sure do. We might have crackheads standing on some of our street corners at night, but we ain't a place where little girls should see their parents killed."

"No place should be," she agreed.

"I don't understand why the cops ain't found the guy responsible. They got that fancy new dog unit and all those fancy trained dogs, and little Lucy is still waiting for justice."

"You know Lucy?"

"Of course I do. Everyone on this street knows her. Cute kid. A shame her parents were losers." He took a cigarette from a pack in his shirt pocket and tapped it against his palm.

"I've heard they may have been killed because they weren't good to her," she said, throwing out one of the reasons she'd heard speculated about on the news.

"Yeah. Well, that's what the talking heads on TV say. You want to know what Buddy Morris says? That's me, by the way." He patted his chest.

"Sure."

"I say they owed someone money."

"Why do you think that?"

His eyes narrowed. "You working with the cops?"

"No. I work for a local cable station."

"But the cops aren't paying you to pick my brains?"

"If they were, would you care? You did say you wanted them to solve the case."

"You've got a point, kid. I do want it solved, and I don't care how the police make that happen. They want to send spies into the neighborhood, that's fine with me."

"I'm not spying. I'm just curious."

"The Emerys were crooks. They made deals and didn't follow through on them. That can get a person killed," Buddy said quietly.

"So, you don't think their murders have anything to do with the way they treated Lucy?"

He shrugged. "Maybe. Maybe not. You want to know more, you should ask CJ. He lives in the house behind theirs."

"CJ? What's his address?"

The man laughed. "Lady, you don't need an address. The Emery place still has yellow bits of tape stuck to the front door. Find it. Walk into the backyard. Go to the chain-link fence and scream his name a couple times. Maybe he'll answer."

"You're not sending her out to CJ's, are you?" one of the other men asked.

"She wants to know what was going on at the Emery place," he responded, the cigarette dangling from his fingers.

"CJ isn't going to talk to her. He doesn't talk to anyone," the man argued, his focus on Sasha. "I'm telling you right now, don't bother. He's not going to talk to you."

"He'll talk to her if she says I sent her." Buddy flicked ashes onto the ground, tossed the cigarette and ground it out with his foot. "You tell him I sent you. He'll talk to you."

"You two are good friends?" Sasha asked, trying to get a feel for how the interpersonal connections worked.

"Wouldn't say we're good friends. I wouldn't even say we're friends. Went to high school together. He doesn't get out, so I bring him groceries once a week. Grab his mail for him. Stuff like that."

"I don't suppose you'd be willing to introduce us?"

He studied her for a moment, his dark

rheumy eyes taking in her running clothes, her scuffed shoes and her empty hands.

"If you'd like some cash for your trouble," she began, knowing she had two twenties tucked into her phone case.

"I don't want your money, lady. I just want you to find that good-news story in our neighborhood and air it."

"I can't promise anything, but I can tell you I will do my best."

"We have a deal," he exclaimed gleefully. "Come on. I got things to do, and I don't want to lollygag around. Of course, I'm sure I'm not as busy as a famous news personality like yourself, Ms. Eastman." He stepped through the gate, walking quickly along the crumbling sidewalk.

"You can call me Sasha. And we both know that I'm far from famous," she said, hoping that maybe this lead would pan out.

She knew how important it was to Bradley that he solve the Emery case. Whatever happened between the two of them, Sasha wanted him to accomplish his goal.

"More famous than me. There it is," Buddy said, pointing toward a dingy house with bits of crime scene tape still dangling from the doorjamb. "The Emery place."

"Did they have a lot of friends?" she asked as they approached the property.

"Probably the same as most people. I used to see them out smoking in their backyard when I dropped stuff off for CJ. Even if they weren't out there, it seemed the kid always was. Rain. Shine. Heat. Cold. Poor kid."

"Did anyone ever live here with them? Like, maybe someone named Andy?" She knew the police had been asking, but she felt compelled to do the same.

"Nah. No Andys. Police keep asking that."

"How about in the neighborhood?"

Buddy rubbed his nearly bald head. "Nope. I know everyone who lives in a five-mile radius, and not one of them is an Andy."

A few houses up the street, a door

opened and a man walked out, a silky-haired brown dachshund in his arms. "Hey, Buddy, what are you doing over there?"

"What's it to you, Vernon?" Buddy replied.

"It's private property. You can't just go traipsing across the yard every time you want to take a shortcut to CJ's house." Vernon hurried across the street, the dog still in his arms.

"That's a funny warning coming from you. Every time I'm here, Brandy's in the yard."

"Brandy?" Sasha asked.

"That thing." He pointed at the dog.

"She isn't a thing," Vernon huffed. "She's a dog, and she's only over here because she's searching for Lucy."

"Guess I can't say anything about that. The kid loved that dog, and the dog loved the kid. It was mutual admiration society. Lucy always said Brandy was her bestest friend." Buddy laughed.

"Her friend?" Sasha repeated, the last

square of the Rubik's Cube suddenly sliding into place.

"Animals can be our friends," Vernon said, a hint of defensiveness in his voice. "And if any human needed a friend, Lucy did. Always wandering around the yard alone. Half the time she was dirty and wearing clothes that weren't appropriate for the weather. Brandy knew she needed someone. I couldn't keep her inside if Lucy was out, and as soon as I opened the door, she'd fly across the street to visit." Vernon patted Brandy's silky head. "She misses her friend."

"Kid use to dress her in doll clothes," Buddy said, smiling at the memory. "Old Vernon here would half-near have a heart attack every time."

"Dogs don't need clothes. Especially not my dog."

"If you thought that, maybe you should have kept the critter in your yard," Buddy replied.

"Maybe you should keep your mouth shut," Vernon responded.

Sasha studied the dog while the two men argued, her mind racing.

She'd listened to the news conferences. She knew the police had been looking for someone named Andy. Andy with brown hair. Who the three-year-old missed.

A three-year-old who might mistake the name Brandy for Andy. Who might not ever mention that the "Andy" was a dog.

"You okay?" Vernon asked, his eyes narrowed.

"Yes. Fine. Just thinking about all the great human-interest stories I might find in this neighborhood."

"That's why you're here?" Vernon asked suspiciously.

"Why else?"

"Nosiness? There's been too many people wandering around asking questions lately. And the police come through every other day, asking the same questions over and over again."

"They want to find the Emerys' murderer," she pointed out, trying to drag her gaze away from the dog.

"Seems to me, those people got what they deserved." Vernon nearly spit the words, his tone filled with venom.

Surprised, Sasha met his mud-brown eyes. "Why do you say that?"

"They didn't take care of their kid. They didn't take care of their property. They didn't take care of their neighbors. Eventually someone decided to take care of them." He let out a snort of laughter. "I got to get back inside. Brandy is waiting on her breakfast."

He hurried away.

Buddy shook his head. "That guy is downright weird."

"Is there a reason you say that?"

"Just a vibe I get. Plus, he doesn't seem to like anyone. As far as I know, he doesn't get along with his neighbors, and he doesn't have any friends. Except his dog. I'm heading around. You'd better stay here. CJ will be more likely to meet with you if you don't go into his yard without permission." He walked through the yard, disappearing around the house.

Sasha stayed put, her heart beating frantically.

She had to be mistaken.

There was no way Andy was a dog named Brandy.

Was there?

She took her phone from her pocket, dialing Bradley's number before she could second-guess herself. He had said he would be in a meeting. Hopefully he would check his voice mail as soon as it was over.

She left a detailed message, explaining what she had discovered and telling him where she was. No apologies. No excuses. If the information was helpful, great. If it wasn't, no harm done.

She shoved the phone in her pocket and tried to see around the side of the house.

She didn't want to get on CJ's bad side. Better to stay out of sight until she was summoned or told to go home.

"No success with CJ yet?"

She jumped, whirling to face Vernon.

He was just steps away. A coat now pulled over his stained T-shirt.

"You scared the life out of me!" she exclaimed.

"Actually, it doesn't seem that I have," he responded. "You're still very much alive and breathing."

She didn't laugh.

She didn't get the impression he wanted her to think it was funny.

"Where's Brandy?"

"In the house eating."

"Shouldn't you be with her?"

"I usually am, but I looked outside and realized that you were still standing here. I thought I'd come back out and find out why."

"I'm thinking of doing a story on the neighborhood," she said. "I work for a local cable show. WBKN. I do feel-good stories about people and places in Brooklyn."

"Nothing feel-good about this neighborhood," he said with a narrow-eyed glare that made her take another step away.

"Look, Vernon, I'm not here to cause any trouble."

He laughed, something evil and ugly just beneath the sound. "Of course you aren't."

"Why would I be?"

"Because you think you're better than we are, walking around in your fancy coat and expensive shoes, acting like you have a right to ask your questions."

"Freedom of speech is a constitutional right, Vernon. I'm not doing any harm by engaging in that right," she replied, suddenly nervous and a little scared. Anxious to get away from Vernon.

"Freedom of speech has gotten people killed, you know that?" he responded.

"I have an appointment soon," she said, glancing at her watch, ready to make her escape.

"Right. A meeting. Like I said, you're too important for this part of town."

"Goodbye, Vernon." She turned away, realizing her mistake a moment too late.

She heard the rustle of fabric and a quick swish of air behind her.

She swung toward the sound, caught a glimpse of something arching through the air.

A heavy baton?

A baseball bat?

She put up her arm and tried to dodge.

The object crashed into her forearm, glancing off her temple with enough force to send her flying backward. She fell, the world spinning. Darkness edging in.

Flying.

Floating.

Realizing she was being carried somewhere.

She managed to open her eyes just enough to see a bright orange car. Vernon opened the trunk, dropping her unceremoniously inside.

"You really should have minded your own business," he grumbled as he shut the trunk.

She lay where she was, allowing her eyes to adjust as the car engine rumbled to life. He was taking her somewhere. She was terrified of what would happen when they reached their destination.

You have your cell phone. Use it! her mind shrieked.

She reached into her vest pocket.

The phone was still there, her fingers clumsy as she pulled it out. Her head was pounding, her arm throbbing, her stomach churning. It hurt to keep her eyes open, but it would hurt more to die before she had a chance to see Bradley again.

She had fallen hard for him.

She didn't know how.

She just knew it had happened.

Everything good she had thought she'd seen in Michael actually existed in Bradley. Kind, generous, gruff and tough, he had a deep love of God, family and justice that shaped everything he did and said. She hadn't been able to resist that.

She didn't want to resist him.

If she got out of this situation alive, she would tell him how she felt. She wouldn't hold back, wouldn't let her fear keep her from pursuing something wonderful.

If she did?

When she did.

The car stopped. Not idling. Stopped cold. She tensed, certain Vernon would open the trunk and finish what he'd started. A minute passed. Two. She thought she heard him walking around the vehicle, his heavy footsteps crunching on gravel or crumbled asphalt.

Where were they?

A park?

She tried to hear past the fear roaring through her head.

Were those waves crashing?

She didn't dare call Bradley again, afraid Vernon was lurking outside and would hear her. Instead, she turned off the sound and texted, grateful she'd left him the detailed voice mail earlier.

Andy/Brandy's owner kidnapped me.

I'm in trunk of orange car.

Maybe near the bay or ocean.

Track cell phone.

Hurry.

She wanted to say more. She wanted to tell him she had fallen in love with him. She wanted to explain how sorry she was that she had let her fear hurt him.

She should have said everything she'd meant, everything she had felt, when she had had the chance. Should have told him just how happy she felt when she was with him and just how eager she was to explore the depth and breadth of their friendship.

She had missed her opportunity.

She could only pray she would have another one.

A quiet click warned her the trunk was about to open.

She hit Send, shoved the phone back into her pocket and closed her eyes, praying desperately that God would show her a way out of the mess she was in.

Sunlight speared her eyes, and Vernon dragged her out by the arm. Her head hit the edge of the trunk, and she stumbled as her feet landed on pavement. She blinked, trying to get her eyes used to the bright light. She hadn't been in the trunk long. They hadn't gone far.

"Where are we?" she asked, her voice shaking. She couldn't stand that. Couldn't stand that this hate-filled man had her so terrified.

"Figure it out yourself," he grumbled.

She glanced around and realized they were at a beach. That was good. A beach meant people. People meant safety. She hoped.

"Vernon, I'm not sure what you think I've done, but if you just leave me here, we can pretend none of this ever happened."

"Shut up! I'm trying to think. This is not where I wanted to be. The docks would have been better. Easier to drown you without someone seeing, but I need gas to get there and money is tight. This'll work. I'll make it work."

"I think—"

"Shut up, I said!" he yelled, flashing the gun that he had hidden beneath his coat. "Or I'll kill you right here, and I won't care who sees."

It had been ten minutes and fifteen seconds since Bradley had received Sasha's voice mail and text. He had tried to call her three times since then. She hadn't answered.

Every available K-9 team was being gathered; a BOLO had been issued for a bright orange car; her cell phone was being actively traced.

Everything that could possibly be done to find her was being done.

It didn't feel like enough.

"Staring at that phone isn't going to make her respond," Henry said, barely looking up from a map he was studying. Vivienne was beside him, placing marks where Sasha's cell phone had pinged.

Near the K-9 unit.

Why hadn't he answered his phone

when she'd called earlier? He'd been about to head into a meeting with his team, trying to figure out how they could finally track down "Andy," while she'd had the information he and the K-9 unit needed. He shook his head, furious at himself. He should have answered.

But he'd figured she'd been calling because she was worried about the way their conversation had ended, and he hadn't been ready to talk about it.

He should have made it clear that he wasn't upset, that he would give her all the time she needed, that he absolutely understood how desperate she was to not be hurt again.

He'd been too anxious for the meeting, hoping for new leads, and to get out on the street and start asking about Andy again.

He thought about the message she'd left. And looked at the text she'd sent.

Andy is a dog named Brandy...

Andy/Brandy's owner kidnapped me.

"Where's Nate?" he asked. Nate was engaged to Lucy's aunt Willow. If anyone could get in touch with her quickly, it was him. He believed Sasha but he wanted the information confirmed.

"Right here," Nate responded, striding across the room with his K-9, Murphy, beside him.

"Can you call Willow? Have her ask Lucy if Andy is a person or a dog?"

Nate's eyes widened, but he didn't ask questions. He knew Sasha had been kidnapped, and he knew time was of the essence.

He pulled out his phone, made the call, his voice terse, his expression grim, and he asked for the information he needed.

When the conversation ended, he met Bradley's eyes.

"Andy is a dog with brown hair. Apparently, Lucy's very best friend."

"A dog?" Henry repeated, looking up from the map. "The guy we've been searching for has fur and can't testify in a court of law?"

"But his owner can," Bradley responded, pushing Play so that the voice mail Sasha had left played again. She was breathless. Apparently unharmed. Giving quick, clear details. The Emerys' house. A neighbor across the street named Vernon with a little brown-haired dog named Brandy.

Suspicious.

Trouble.

May need help.

The words skipped and tumbled through his head, adrenaline pumping through him.

"We need to find her. Now," he muttered.

King whined, sensing his tension and fear.

"We will," Vivienne assured him. "This map is leading us straight to her." She pointed to the marks she'd made. "Cell phone tower pings all the way to Manhattan Beach. She's been there for a little over twenty minutes."

Bradley's stomach churned. Manhattan Beach again. Bad guys liked the place.

Desolate spots and an ocean to dump their victims. "Let's pray she stays there for another twenty more," Bradley said, grabbing his coat and heading for the door.

The sergeant grabbed his arm, pulling him to a stop.

"I understand why you want to rush, but I want to remind you that a sloppy plan leads to a sloppy outcome."

"Sloppy plan?" Nate said. "We don't have any plan at all."

"Exactly," Gavin agreed. "We can take five minutes to hash it through, come up with the best message of approach and then move in. The last thing we want is for Sasha to be injured."

"The last thing we want," Penny said loudly from her desk, "is for Sasha to die."

"So, let's be clear-thinking. If they're on the beach, what approach is going to keep us out of sight?"

"There are plenty of people who walk the beach this time of year. I'll just go out there and pretend to be enjoying the view," Penny offered. "Once I'm close enough—"

"No," Bradley said harshly. "You aren't trained, and we don't need more civilians involved."

Her eyes flashed and her lips tightened, but she must have realized now wasn't the time to argue. "I suppose you have a better plan?"

"Every K-9 officer dresses as a civilian. We go in plain clothes, surround the orange car and take this guy down. Until we actually see where the vehicle is and understand the situation better, that's about as good as it's going to get."

Gavin frowned. "I hate to agree, but if this guy murdered the Emerys—"

"He did," Bradley cut in.

"If he did, he's already killed once. There's nothing keeping him from killing again. Everyone understand what we're doing?"

The team gave agreement as a group.

"Good. Go to your lockers. Change. Do whatever you need to do to not look like a K-9 police officer. We'll meet back here in ten. Head out immediately."

The group took off, everyone moving quickly.

Bradley should have been relieved.

All he felt was terror.

A murderer had Sasha.

Every minute that ticked away was another opportunity for him to hurt her.

It took him five minutes to change out of his suit into casual clothes he kept in his locker. Less to get King out of his work vest. He kept the same lead and collar. Just as he would if he were working undercover. King understood what that meant. He knew he was still on the job, and he pranced excitedly as he waited, whining under his breath every few minutes.

"I know, boy. I want to leave, too," Bradley said, his voice husky with concern and fear.

"It's going to be okay, Bradley," Penelope said, wrapping her arm around his waist and offering a quick, firm hug. He had been her protector, her mentor, her supporter for as long as he could remember, offering advice, lending an ear, giving her a shoulder to cry on when she needed it.

Now she was an adult. A strong, accomplished woman who knew her mind and her heart, and who was now offering him the things that he had spent so many years giving her.

"I hope so," he said.

"You should know so," Henry said as he stepped into the room. "Our entire team is working on this. Our track record for success is excellent."

"It is," Gavin agreed as he joined them.

Within minutes the remainder of the team had returned, dogs out of vests, uniforms off, guns hidden beneath their coats. Ready to do what they did best. To work as a team, to protect the innocent and to bring justice to the guilty.

Gavin gave one last brief, reiterating the need to be careful, cautious and aware. They had pinned down the location of the orange car. A patrol officer had confirmed that it was in the parking lot near Manhattan Beach Park.

Now all they had to do was get there, and then use the dogs to track down Sasha and the man who had kidnapped her.

"Ready?" Gavin asked. "Let's head out."

Bradley didn't wait for a second invitation.

He was in his Jeep and heading for the beach before most of the team had left the building.

Sasha was in danger.

He was going to do whatever was necessary to save her.

TWELVE

Sasha was digging her own grave.

She knew it but could do nothing about it.

Vernon was standing a few inches away, watching as she scooped another shovelful of sand and tossed it toward the lush tree that shaded the area.

In late spring or early summer, the park would have been too crowded for this. Every bit of sand taken up by humanity. There would have been families and laughter, games of beach volleyball and rows of sunbathers. As far as beaches went, this stretch of sand was small, the area more for the community of Manhattan Beach than for tourists who flocked to the other beaches during the hottest summer months.

In the fall, it was empty except for a few die-hard beachcombers, runners and dog walkers.

"How about you spend a little more time digging and a little less time daydreaming?" Vernon snapped, the gun still tucked under his coat. She could see the barrel poking toward her beneath the fabric. If he shot her now, someone would see him. He certainly couldn't push her into the pit she was digging and bury her without garnering attention.

"I'm trying, but I'm sick from that knock on my head, and I think my arm is broken." She lifted her left arm. The area below her wrist was black-and-blue, the skin tight from swelling.

"And?" he asked dispassionately.

"It's difficult to dig quickly when you're only using one hand."

"Then use two and deal with the pain. Either that or don't. We'll just go back to the car, and I'll bring you to a place where no one is going to notice if and when I shoot you. Any alley will be fine. I can toss you in a dumpster, and it may take days for anyone to find you." He scowled. "That should have been my first plan. I'd be done with you by now."

"You're asking me to dig my own grave, Vernon," she said, hoping there might be some compassion in him, a bit of humanity that would make him rethink his choices.

He laughed. "Do you think I'm that stupid? There aren't many people around, but there are enough. Right now, all you're doing is digging sand for a nice big sand sculpture. If anyone remembers me here, that's what I'm going to tell them."

"And? Then what?" she asked, tossing another shovelful of sand to the side.

"I haven't decided yet. Tragic accident when the sand caves in on you? Tragic drowning when you accidentally fall off the pier? I think deaths should be appropriate to the person. Don't you?"

"Sure," she agreed, eyeing the surrounding area. If she ran, would he shoot and hope that he wasn't seen? "But I have never done anything to hurt you. And there is no need for either of those things to happen."

"That's my decision. Not yours. And I don't like nosy people. Ridding the world of one is a favor to the cosmos."

"I'm a journalist. It's my job to be nosy," she argued. Good thing she *was* because she'd set her phone to record while she was still in the trunk. If she could get Vernon to confess to killing the Emerys before he killed her, at least the K-9 unit would have that. The thought made her shiver and she purposely tripped over the pile of dirt she'd removed, causing a good amount of it to fall back in the hole.

It would be very easy to stage an accident like the ones Vernon had described. People drowned every year. People died when sand pits caved in. Beaches were lovely, but they could be dangerous. She shuddered.

She wasn't afraid to die.

She had just been hoping to do it a little later in life.

"Be careful!" Vernon bellowed. "We don't have time to redo this."

"We? I'm the one doing all the work." She purposely goaded him, hoping to distract him and make him focus on something other than the timeline he had in his head.

She had to believe that Bradley had gotten her messages and her texts. She had to believe that he and his team were on the way to help.

She just had to slow down the process of being murdered.

She needed to stay alive long enough to be saved. She knew that not getting caught was everything to Vernon. He could have easily dragged her into his house, killed her there and then stuffed her in a suitcase to get rid of her body later. He clearly wanted no evidence in his own home that she'd been there. Perhaps he was even hoping to make her death look accidental. Anything to throw the police off his trail.

She could use his fear of being caught

to her advantage, manipulate his fears. Somehow.

"Please, God," she prayed out loud, hoping Vernon might feel a twinge of guilt. "Help me."

"No one is going to help you, lady. So shut up and keep working."

"You don't have to kill me."

"Sure I do."

"Why?"

"You know my secret."

"All I know is that you have a dog named Brandy."

"You know Lucy called her Andy. You know that my dog is the man the cops have been looking for." He cackled gleefully. "It's been a riot watching them canvass the neighborhood looking for some guy with brown hair named Andy. You know they even brought Lucy out one day?"

"No," she said, swallowing down bile as she scooped up more dirt.

"They did. Drove her up and down the streets hoping she would spot her special friend. I heard about it before they reached my street. Brandy and I stayed inside that day."

"You have to know that they'll find you eventually. Buddy and Gunner both know you're the last person to see me alive."

He scowled. "Those guys won't talk to the cops. Why would they? They don't really know you, so they won't care about you one way or the other. But they did know the Emerys. And those two were low-level criminals. They cheated everyone they dealt with. They neglected their kid. They let a nice house go to ruin. Got away with it for years, too. They'd still be getting away with it if I hadn't stopped them. The way I see it, the community owes me a favor for killing the Emerys."

There it was. The confession. And it was all caught on her phone, recording in her pocket.

"Then go home and ask them to throw you a party. Leave me alone. I won't say anything to anyone about this."

"Of course you will. You're a reporter.

You can't help yourself. Dig faster. There are some people on the beach over there. I wouldn't want to have to kill them, too."

Terrified, she glanced in the direction he was looking.

A woman was walking her dog near the water's edge. Closer to the parking lot, someone else was throwing a ball for his...

Malinois?

Her heart skipped a beat, her gaze dropping quickly.

They were there, and she knew if she looked around she would see more team members, slowly moving closer, trying to get an opportunity to take Vernon down before he could fire the gun.

"Dig faster," he growled, and she scooped another shovelful. A dog suddenly appeared. A beagle. Brown, white and black with a sweet face and a wagging tail, heading right for her.

Cody!

If he was there, Henry was, too.

"Get away!" Vernon snapped, stamping a foot in Cody's direction. Undaunted, the beagle kept coming, his tail wagging wildly as he watched the shovel.

He thought Sasha was playing a game, and he was excited to play, too.

"No. Stay." She tried to stop him, but he just kept coming, his lean body moving like he had all the time in the world.

"I said, get away," Vernon shouted, raising the gun, pointing it.

She couldn't let it happen.

She swung the shovel at his head, too weak from her injuries to get much force behind it.

He grabbed the handle, twisting it from her hand and tossing it away.

"Die!" he said quietly. Coldly. Then he lifted the gun and pointed it straight at her heart.

She braced for what she knew was coming, praying that God would make it painless, that He would watch over the people she was leaving behind. Coworkers. Friends. The K-9 unit that had worked so diligently to keep her safe.

Bradley.

Because she wanted him to always be happy, to always have joy in his life.

Instead of a gunshot, she heard a vicious snarl and saw a flurry of tan and black launching through the air.

The gun went off as King latched on to Vernon's gun arm and dragged him to the ground, shaking him until the gun fell from his grip.

Vernon howled, his cries ringing through the air and mixing with the wild screams of the gulls.

In seconds, it was over.

Vernon cuffed and lying facedown on the ground.

King still snarling as Bradley called him back.

Sasha stumbled a few steps away, collapsing onto the warm, soft sand, her head pounding, her arm throbbing, her heart soaring with gratefulness.

"Are you okay?" Bradley asked, crouching beside her, his dark eyes filled with concern.

"I am now," she responded, wrapping her hand around his and looking into his eyes. "I'm sorry," she said.

"Sorry? You deserve an award for finally giving us the information we needed to bring this guy down."

"Not for that," she murmured, watching as the sergeant pulled a wallet from Vernon's pocket, opened it up and read his ID.

"Vernon Parker, huh?"

"What's it to you?" Vernon spit.

"Not much. Just wanted to know whose name we're writing on the paperwork. Vernon Parker, you're under arrest for attempted murder." He read Vernon his Miranda rights before dragging him to his feet. "And in case you think that will be the only charge, we'll be filing murder charges, too. We have no doubt that your DNA will match evidence our forensic scientist has been painstakingly working to retrieve from evidence found at the Emery crime scene back in April."

"You're crazy. I would never hurt anyone," Vernon protested.

"You're saying that while you stand three feet from the grave you were making me dig for myself," Sasha pointed out. "Oh, and guess what? The phone in my pocket recorded your confession to killing the Emerys and why."

He lunged toward her, nearly breaking free of Gavin's hold.

"Let's go," Gavin said, dragging him away. "Good job, Ms. Eastman," he called over his shoulder.

"Very good job," Bradley said, holding her gaze. "That was some excellent detective work on your part. We were working on finding Andy for months and you're the one who uncovered that Andy was really Brandy—and a dog. I didn't realize how closely related our skills are."

She smiled, appreciating his praise, but she was still too shaken to think beyond being safe.

"We should get out of here, too." Bradley helped her to her feet, slid his arm around her waist. "Are you sure you're okay?"

"I will be," she replied.

"Looks like you might need an X-ray." He touched her arm.

"I don't think it's broken. Some ice and some ibuprofen, and I'll be fine."

"You might be, but I'll spend the next few days worrying that something is broken or bleeding internally."

"You have too much on your plate to worry about me."

"Like?"

"Your job. All the people in Brooklyn who count on you and the K-9 unit."

"My job is important to me. I'll admit it takes up a lot of my thoughts, but you are always on my mind, too. And now that we've made progress on the Emery case, I'll have more than enough time to focus on worrying about your health and well-being."

She looked into his eyes, saw the humor and relief there.

"You know what?"

"What?"

"I really do like you, Detective Mc-Gregor."

He laughed. "Good. So, how about we get you checked out while my colleagues take Vernon in for questioning?"

"This is your case. You need to be there."

"I'll be there when they book him for murder and when he is convicted and tossed into prison, where he belongs."

"If it happens." She frowned. She knew how the criminal justice system worked. Even airtight cases could be lost.

"I have no doubt it will. Between the confession you have on your phone and the DNA evidence our forensic scientist will likely be able to match, we'll be able to close it fast and, hopefully, get him to plead guilty."

"Since when are you the optimist in this relationship?" she joked, then realized how it sounded. "What I mean is—"

"I hope what you mean is what you said. I like the idea of a relationship with you. Now. How about that X-ray?"

"Only if you drive me to the hospital. I'm not keen on another ambulance ride this month."

"It's a deal," he said, calling to King as he helped her across the beach, the bright sunshine dancing on the waves, gulls calling wildly, King chasing waves and birds. K-9 officers huddled in groups, discussing the successful rescue, the capture of a murderer they'd been hunting for seven months. She could see their smiles, feel their joy, and all of it was so breathtakingly perfect, tears filled her eyes.

"You're crying," Bradley said quietly, stopping to study her face, his palms cupping her cold cheeks, his touch as gentle as his gaze. "Are you in more pain than you told me?"

"No."

"Then why the tears?" he asked, brushing one from her cheek.

"Relief, I guess," she said, glancing at the beach and the men, women and dogs she had come to admire, respect and care about. "And joy."

"Because you're alive?" he asked, a tender smile curving his lips.

"Because I'm surrounded by the family I never thought I'd have, looking into the eyes of the only man I've ever truly loved, and it feels like I have finally found a place where I belong."

"We are your people, huh?"

"You are my person," she corrected.

He leaned down so that they were eye to eye, his forehead resting against hers, his palms still warm against her cheeks. "And you're mine. I love you, Sasha. More than I ever imagined I could love anyone."

He kissed her then, his lips warm, his hands gentle, and she knew that if she lived a hundred more years, she would remember the way it felt to feel so cherished, valued and loved.

"You're an extraordinary woman, Sasha," he whispered against her lips. "And I'm going to spend the rest of my life thanking God for bringing you into my life."

He stepped back, allowing his hands to

drop away. "But first, I'm bringing you to the hospital."

Sasha laughed, taking his hand as they walked to his Jeep, all the heartache and pain of the past forgotten, and she stepped toward the future God had planned for her.

EPILOGUE

Sasha had never been part of a large Thanksgiving celebration. Even as a child, before her mother's murder, Thanksgiving Day had consisted of their small family gathering around the kitchen table, thanking God for their blessings before they ate the meal her parents had prepared. As an adult, she had avoided attending Thanksgiving meals with coworkers or friends. Not because she didn't see the value in doing so, but because the people she knew had families and relatives who would fill their homes and make the day complete.

She hadn't wanted to be an add-on or an extra.

She had wanted to belong.

And now she did.

Her heart swelled at the thought as she stepped into the large meeting room that the K-9 unit was using for their Thanksgiving meal. Not just any Thanksgiving meal. This was a celebration of the closing of the Emery murder investigation, and the entire unit would be there. Bradley had invited Sasha, and she hadn't even considered saying no. After years of side-stepping invitations and making excuses, she was finally going to be part of a wonderful time of thanksgiving and praise.

"Sasha! You made it!" Bradley said, moving through a small crowd of people and dogs that were congregated in the middle of the room.

"It looks like I'm a little late," she murmured, allowing him to take the covered dish she had brought from her apartment. Her mother's dressing. She had found the recipe in an old cookbook stored in the back of her closet.

"There are plenty of people still on the way, and you are right on time," he responded, kissing her sweetly, gently. Right there in front of the members of the K-9 unit and all their loved ones. "And I am very glad to see you."

"You saw me three hours ago when you stopped by to tell me that Darcy Fields finally extracted DNA evidence from the doorknob at the Emerys' crime scene and that it matched Vernon's," she reminded him, smiling into his eyes, her heart filled to overflowing with gratefulness. She hadn't expected to fall in love again. She hadn't wanted to. But she didn't regret it. She didn't doubt it.

She knew that Bradley was the man she was meant to love. He was her friend, her partner in beach exploration and late-night conversations. His loyalty, his passion for truth and justice, his love for his sister, his friends, for King and for Sasha, were undeniable, and she couldn't have liked or admired him more if she had tried.

Love was the frosting on the cake of happiness they had found with one another. She couldn't deny it any more than she could deny the sunrise in the morning or the dusky blue of the sky when the sun set at night.

"Three hours is a long time to be away from someone you love," he said as he took her hand and led her to a buffet table laden with covered dishes.

"It smells great in here," she murmured, her stomach growling loudly.

"Hungry?" he asked with a smile.

"Always," she replied, laughing as King nosed the edge of the table, sniffing loudly as he tried to determine what was there. "I think King is, too."

"Looks like the last few people are here," he said, pointing to the door.

Penny and her fiancé, Tyler, walked in.

"Hello, brother!" Penny called, rushing over to hug Bradley.

"And Sasha," she added, offering Sasha a hug, as well.

"Looks like we're all here," Sergeant Gavin Sutherland said, his springer spaniel Tommy prancing near his feet as he approached the front of the room. "Before I offer the blessing on this Thanksgiving feast, I want to thank each and every one of you for the hard work you do for the team. You are vital assets to the K-9 unit and to the New York City Police Department. Thanks to your efforts, we have finally solved the Emery murder investigation."

He glanced to his right, and Sasha realized Willow Emery, little Lucy Emery's aunt, was there, Detective Nate Slater's arm wrapped around her waist, his dog Murphy near her feet. Lucy was a few feet away, sitting at a child-sized table coloring in a coloring book.

"I know that Willow is grateful for your effort in making that happen. And I want to share some news I received early this morning. The perpetrator of that crime, Vernon Parker, was told about the DNA evidence we found at the scene. Faced with that and the taped confession obtained by Sasha, he agreed through his lawyer to plead guilty."

"Thank You, Lord," Willow said quietly,

leaning her head against Nate's shoulder. "We'll be saved from a long trial."

A murmur of agreement filled the room, couples talking quietly about the case and about the newest development.

"It's over," Sasha said quietly, her arm slipping around Bradley's waist.

"As close as it can be before he is sentenced and locked away," Bradley agreed. "It's been a long seven months. I think everyone on the unit will sleep well tonight."

"A long seven months that accomplished a lot of things for a lot of people," she replied, scanning the faces of people she had come to know and love. Not just people. Couples who had come together because of the work the K-9 unit had done. Henry Roarke and Olivia Vance. Raymond Morrow and Karenna Pressley. Vivienne Armstrong and Caleb Black. Belle Montera and Emmett Gage. Jackson Davison and Darcy Fields. Penny and Nate.

"I hope they all have their happily-ever-afters," she said.

"They will," Bradley assured her, not

asking what she meant. He knew. They had talked about the people in the unit many times, and they had both been awed by the way God had brought love into so many of their lives.

"You say that with authority, Detective McGregor. So I'll assume you're right," she responded.

He laughed quietly, his dark eyes soft and filled with love. "I'm glad you think so," he said, taking both her hands and looking straight into her eyes. "Because there is something else I plan to be right about."

"What's that?" she asked, the room suddenly quiet, all the attention focused on them. No one spoke. Even the dogs had gone quiet, the soft swish of their tails against the floor the only sound.

"We'll have our happily-ever-after, too," Bradley said, all the amusement gone from his eyes and face. "If you want one."

"I can't think of anything I want more," she admitted, all the fear she'd once had, all the certainty that she would spend the rest of her life alone, gone. Love was not a scary thing. Not when it was made of friendship and kindness and respect and faith, all of it bound with hope.

"I hope you know how much I love you, Sasha. Not just for today, but forever, I want to stand beside you. Through the good and bad. The hard and the easy. Every day. For as long as I have breath in my lungs and life in my chest. Will you marry me?"

He reached into his pocket and pulled out a small box, opening it to reveal a simple rose-cut solitaire, the band a braided ribbon of gold.

"Yes," she said, her throat clogged with tears, her voice raspy with love and hope and joy.

The room exploded in cheers and barks and howls of joy, everyone moving closer as Bradley slipped the ring on her finger.

She knew people were talking, issuing congratulations, but all she could see was Bradley, all she could hear were his words as his lips brushed hers.

"You are my forever. My happily-ever-after. The place I will always call home. Today and every day, I thank God that He brought you into my life."

Then he was kissing her with passion and with promise. And, for today and for always, she was grateful.

* * * * *

If you enjoyed this series,
return to the Brooklyn K-9 Unit with
True Blue K-9 Unit:
Brooklyn Christmas
by Laura Scott and Maggie K. Black,
available December 2020
from Love Inspired Suspense.

Dear Reader,

The interesting thing about the past is that it is always with us. Days, week, years, decades later, we still carry memories of both good and bad times. Those memories, as well as the experiences that created them, shape us for the better or for the worse. As the True Blue K-9 Unit: Brooklyn series has unfolded, you've met many characters impacted by the Emery and McGregor murders. Though the crimes happened twenty years apart, the similarities between them dredged up the past and rekindled the desire for justice that Bradley McGregor carried since he was a fourteen-year-old suspect in his parents' deaths. Although his sister, Penny, was too young to remember many details of life before the murders of their parents, Bradley remembers a lot. Those experiences have shaped him into the man he has become.

As I wrote his and Sasha Eastman's

story, I couldn't help thinking about my past. The weight of my mistakes, my hurts, my disappointments can often be difficult to carry. As a survivor of domestic violence and a woman who went to church every Sunday with her abuser, there have been times when the past has seemed too heavy to bear. The fear and anxiety that dogs survivors of traumatic experiences can be overwhelming, and we often struggle to hold on to our faith and to believe that there are better and brighter times ahead. But God…

Savior. Redeemer. Friend. Author of new beginnings. Ever-present help in troubled times.

The world is filled with darkness, heartache and pain, but God is the great physician, the steadfast helper and guide. He brings light into the darkest places and peace into the most troubled souls. He doesn't shout, demand or threaten. He whispers to our hearts: *Come to me, all you who are weary and burdened, and I will give you rest. Take my yoke upon you and learn from me, for I am gentle and humble in heart, and you will find rest for your weary souls.*

Whatever your heartaches, I pray His peace into your life. May there be renewed hope in every breath you take.

I enjoy interacting with readers. You can find me on Facebook, Twitter and Instagram. Or drop me a line at shirleermccoy@hotmail.com.

Blessings,

Shirlee McCoy